She Dre~~~~ Looked at Him.

As she started to turn away, he caught her shoulders.

"Was it there?" His voice was low, barely a whisper.

"What?"

"Whatever it was you were looking for."

"No."

"Oh, it's there. You just didn't look far enough. Care to try again?"

Casey knew she should walk away. She should shout no at the top of her lungs and run before it was too late. But the mere touch of his hands on her shoulders was her undoing.

She melted against him and raised her lips to his.

RUTH LANGAN
says her biggest downfall is reading. "I read when I should be writing." Luckily, she still manages to find time for her work as a writer and for her husband and five children.

Dear Reader,

Although our culture is always changing, the desire to love and be loved is a constant in every woman's heart. Silhouette Romances reflect that desire, sweeping you away with books that will make you laugh and cry, poignant stories that will move you time and time again.

This summer we're featuring Romances with a playful twist. Remember those fun-loving heroines who always manage to get themselves into tricky predicaments? You'll enjoy reading about their escapades in Silhouette Romances by Brittany Young, Debbie Macomber, Annette Broadrick and Rita Rainville.

We're also publishing Romances by many of your all-time favorites such as Ginna Gray, Dixie Browning, Laurie Paige and Joan Hohl. Your overwhelming reaction to these authors has served as a touchstone for us, and we're pleased to bring you more books with Silhouette's distinctive medley of charm, wit and—above all—*romance*. I hope you enjoy this book, and the many stories to come.

Sincerely,

Rosalind Noonan
Editor
SILHOUETTE BOOKS

SRRL-7/85

RUTH LANGAN
This Time Forever

Silhouette Romance

Published by Silhouette Books New York

America's Publisher of Contemporary Romance

To Pat and Marg
More than sisters . . . friends.

SILHOUETTE BOOKS
300 E. 42nd St., New York, N.Y. 10017

ISBN: 0-373-08371-8

First Silhouette Books printing July 1985

10 9 8 7 6 5 4 3 2 1

America's Publisher of Contemporary Romance

Printed in the U.S.A.

Books by Ruth Langan

Silhouette Romance

Silhouette Special Edition

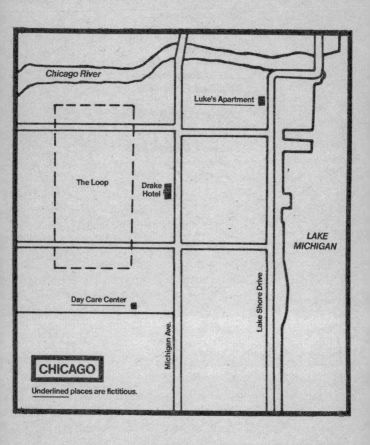

Chicago River

Luke's Apartment

The Loop

Drake Hotel

LAKE MICHIGAN

Day Care Center

Michigan Ave.

Lake Shore Drive

CHICAGO

Underlined places are fictitious.

Chapter One

"This isn't at all what I expected."

Luke Pierson switched off the ignition of the Mercedes, tense from fighting Chicago's noontime traffic from the Loop clear across town. He studied the sprawling old house beyond the wrought-iron fence. Made of stone and brick, like an English country estate, it looked faded among the more glittering contemporary houses and condominiums. Still, Luke decided grudgingly, it had a sort of old-world charm.

His secretary had raved about this day-care center, and the cheerful, dedicated woman who headed the staff of elderly assistants. Somehow, in his mind, he had pictured a clinic, not this comfortable old place surrounded by a rolling lawn and budding fruit trees.

Bright afternoon sun glinted off the silver hood of the

car, and Luke squinted behind his sunglasses. Taking a deep drag on the cigarette, he expelled the smoke in a thin stream. He gave an impatient glance at his watch and scowled. With quick, abrupt movements, he stubbed out the cigarette, opened the car door, and strode toward the front gate. With a critical eye he noted the modern touches that had been added to the old building. A section of the porch had been ramped for easy access. Inside, he glanced at the ceiling and noted with satisfaction that the building was equipped with smoke alarms and a complete sprinkler system.

The screen door was unlocked. Luke stepped inside and into a small foyer. Dark hardwood floors gleamed with a patina of years of careful polish. An ageless grandfather clock chimed the half hour. This room spoke of a home, well lived in, much loved. Not an institution, and certainly not any day-care center he had seen. Luke was aware of the scent of lemon furniture polish and, beyond, the muted sounds of children's laughter and music.

He peered into a room located just off the foyer, and his glance moved slowly over two toddlers playing under the watchful eye of an elderly woman, sitting in a rocker, in a bright floral dress. In the corner, a huge mound of black fur reclined; with one eye blinking lazily, a shaggy dog provided a cushion for a little girl who snuggled contentedly against its neck. For a brief moment, the animal lifted its nose, sniffed halfheartedly, then dropped its head to doze.

Luke frowned at the casual disorder of the room. A pile of wooden blocks lay scattered near the doorway. In front of the fireplace, where a fire crackled invitingly, a child's patterned quilt lay in a heap. On a low, round table, cookie crumbs and napkins were all that remained of a snack. He glanced once more at the scene in the corner. Big, hairy dogs didn't belong in day-care centers, Luke thought with a trace of irritation. They belonged in kennels, behind fences.

He stalked down the hall toward another room. He was beginning to have strong misgivings about this whole setup. Despite the way his secretary had praised this place and its staff, he had the impression of a very laid-back, almost lazy approach to child care.

A fat, white cat circled his leg, leaving a trail of hair clinging to his dark slacks. He glanced down in surprise, then looked up to meet the alert black eyes of a sparse, stooped woman.

"I'm looking for Ms. Leary."

Black eyes snapped up and down his figure, examining him intently, before she responded.

"She isn't here yet. Should be back in a minute."

"Where is her office?"

Again, that steady look before she shrugged. "Her office is down that hallway, then to the left."

"Thank you. I'll wait for her." He nodded and walked briskly away.

He passed a nursery, with four cribs and shelves of stuffed animals. The air smelled of baby powder.

On a door marked C. LEARY, Luke paused, turned the knob, then entered.

A vase of bright yellow daffodils spread golden sunshine in a corner of the room. Loudly proclaiming spring, they brightened a plain gray file cabinet. The desk top was littered with papers and notes. In the midst of the clutter stood a small vase with a single spray of lilacs. Their heady scent filled the room. He picked up an antique paperweight and studied the winter scene, complete with falling snow. For a brief moment it reminded him of an old kindergarten teacher he had loved.

Luke stalked to the window, impatient to be done with this necessary intrusion into his tight schedule. He may as well write off lunch, he thought. He'd never make it now. Where did the days go? The weeks? How long could he stay on this treadmill before it caugh up with him?

He shook a cigarette from a pack and held a gold lighter to the trip. As he blew out a stream of smoke, he watched a slim, boyish figure scurry along the sidewalk, juggling two overflowing grocery bags. Maybe he ought to consider delivery service, he mused. It would eliminate the need to stop at the grocery store after work.

Casey Leary nudged her way through the door, balancing the bags precariously. Using her hip and her elbow, she managed to close the door behind her.

"Here. Gimme those." Two gnarled hands reached for the bags, and Casey relaxed her grip.

"Thanks, Vern. I wasn't sure I'd make it." She smiled affectionately at the stocky handyman whose white hair spilled about a deeply lined, ruddy face.

"You should've told me. I'd have gone along to help."

"Sure. While you fixed that leaky faucet and replaced the cracked window." She grinned and picked up a little girl who stood, her arms outstretched, waiting to be cuddled. "Hi, Punkin," she murmured, planting a kiss on her cheek. Swinging the little girl to her feet, Casey followed the old man through the foyer toward the back of the house.

A warm spring sun slanted through the windows, showing an occasional smudge from childish fingers. Casey made a mental note to pick up a fresh bottle of window cleaner next time she went to the store. The rays of the sun diffused through the upper window-panes, bathing her in a shaft of light, seeking out all the russet highlights in her lush brown hair and turning the ends to flame.

Patience Cranston poked her head in the doorway. Her dark eyes glittered with humor. "You've got a visitor in your office."

Casey thought a moment. "I don't have any appointments today. Do you think it's another city inspector?"

"Not this one. Tall, dark, handsome, in a mysterious sort of way. Kind of sexy, if you like silent, scowling types." There was a gleam of mischief that Casey recognized. Patience was constantly trying to play Cupid.

"Why didn't you just give him an appointment and send him on his way?"

One eyebrow arched over the black eyes. "This one didn't look like the type who would leave unless he wanted to. I've seen his kind before. Tangled with a few, too, when I was younger."

Casey gave a deep sigh of resignation before handing the little girl to Patience and turning away. As she walked toward her office, she reached up to slick back the errant strands of hair. Frowning at her slim, faded jeans, she brushed furiously at the baby powder that dusted the front of her sweater. Why couldn't these people come to see her on the weekends, when she took care of all her appointments? And, she thought wryly, when she was properly dressed in a business suit.

He was standing with his back to the doorway, scrutinizing the framed degrees on the wall. There was tension in the way he stood; he fairly crackled with electricity. He was tall—at least six feet, she figured, measuring her nearly five feet three inches against his height. His suit was dark, and expertly tailored to fit wide, athletic shoulders and trim, narrow hips. Coal-black hair was professionally styled—very short, razor sharp. She glanced down. His shoes were of imported Italian leather, and polished to a high sheen. This was definitely no city inspector. Yet he seemed unlike any executive she had dealt with. His profile was hard, as though chiseled from granite.

When he turned, she felt momentarily stunned. He was a commanding presence. There was a casual arrogance about him. His face wasn't handsome in the classic sense; his jaw was a bit too firm, the cheekbones hollow, etched with a shadow of something. Pain? Anger? His eyes were gray; hard, like steel. Long, sooty lashes softened the image, but just barely. She sensed a simmering temper in those depths, a carefully controlled hostility. For the briefest moment she wondered if the anger was directed at her or at the world in general.

"Hello. I'm Casey Leary." As she extended her hand, she realized she had taken him by surprise with that simple statement.

Quickly composing himself, he accepted her handshake. "Luke Pierson," he said.

His voice was deep, rich. It was the sort of perfectly modulated voice she heard on news broadcasts. A slight regional drawl. Southwest, she figured. Just the right inflection. This man, she knew instinctively, was accustomed to speaking his mind and having others listen without interruption.

She caught the look that skimmed her from head to toe. His gaze paused a moment at the powder that still clung to the front of her sweater before returning to meet her eyes. Withdrawing her hand, she quickly moved behind her desk, hoping it would give her the proper air of authority.

He realized with a start that she was the one he had watched walking down the sidewalk, delivering groceries. Although she was small and slim, he noticed soft curves beneath the rose-colored sweater. She smelled faintly of baby powder. It suited her.

He watched the way the sunlight streamed through the window and caught her in its rays. Her hair was so many different colors that he couldn't pinpoint just what to call it. It was a warm reddish-brown, with blond and russet strands. Her eyes were hazel, nearly amber in the bright sun. She had a direct, honest way of looking at him that was unsettling. In fact, he thought with a jolt, there was a lot about this woman that was unsettling.

Casey forced herself to relax as he studied her. Even at ease, there seemed to be something dangerous about him.

"You're younger than I expected," he said, taking

the chair she indicated. He stretched his long legs out in front of him, crossing them casually at the ankle.

She was quick to note the relaxed pose, at odds with the tension that seemed to emanate from him in waves. She lifted an eyebrow. At twenty-five, with all the years of university training behind her, she didn't feel young or inexperienced. There were few people who could intimidate her. But she knew that her appearance was deceiving.

"Really. What did you expect?"

Luke motioned to the array of framed documents. "Everything here except a PhD. Very impressive. I guess I expected a prim, bespectacled child psychologist."

She inclined her head without comment, waiting to hear why he wanted to see her.

He made a steeple of his hands and watched her intently. "I'm new to the Chicago area."

"Where are you from?"

"Dallas."

She had been right about the drawl. "Oh, that's such a nice city. I spent a wonderful month there once."

He liked her smile. It touched her eyes and gave her a warm radiance. In the sunlight he could see little flecks of green around the pupil. Cat's eyes. That hair would be as soft as a cat's, too. And her skin. The thought jolted him. He forced his thoughts back to the reason for this visit.

He nodded. "I'm with Pierson-Farris. Do you know it?"

"I'm afraid not. Is it a law firm?" She wondered what legal entanglement she was going to find herself in.

"Oil," he said simply. "Our Midwest branch is involved in seeking out new oil deposits and obtaining mineral rights."

She waited, knowing that, in some roundabout fashion, this was leading to his reason for being here without the courtesy of a prior appointment.

He took a breath and met her cool gaze. "Ms. Leary, I have a three-year-old son, Danny. I need a competent day-care service. My secretary, Denise Carver, couldn't say enough good things about you."

"I see." She stared at her desk top before meeting his look. "Mr. Pierson, I'm very flattered that I'm beginning to gain a good reputation. However, at this time I'm afraid we're filled to capacity. I'd be more than happy to put your name on the waiting list. I'm sure . . ."

"You don't understand," he interrupted impatiently. "I need someone immediately. I've been here two weeks, and I've already gone through three baby-sitters."

"I'm sorry that you're having such a bad time of it, Mr. Pierson. But there's really nothing I can do about it."

When he opened his mouth to speak, she held up a hand. It was a delicate hand, he noted, with long, tapered fingers. An artist's hand. A creative hand.

"Maybe you didn't notice, but all my assistants are elderly. I have a theory that older, retired men and women bring a great many skills and experience to these children that younger, less patient people don't possess. Most of my employees come from senior-citizen complexes or retirement villages. Because of their age, I will only take on one child per assistant. That's all they can manage while still giving each child enough of their time and attention."

"Then hire another assistant," he snapped.

Her eyes narrowed. The arrogance of the hard-driving, cynical types of this world never ceased to amaze her. "It isn't that simple. I've been in this business less than a year. I'm progressing, but very slowly. I can't afford to hire another assistant at this time."

She didn't add that she was constantly forced to dip into her grandmother's trust to make ends meet. The insurance premiums were astronomical. Added to that were the van she had purchased, the changes the city had demanded in the house before permitting her to obtain a license, and the salaries of the wonderful people who lavished so much love on their young charges. And there was the cost of maintaining this once elegant old house.

His lips thinned. "I'll make it worth your while, Ms. Leary." He reached into his upper pocket and withdrew a check. With a flourish, he signed his name and dropped the check on her desk.

She glanced at it, then looked up at him without a word.

"It's a blank check, Ms. Leary. Fill in the amount you need to hire another employee." His manner was so brusque, his tone so pompous, she wanted to tear up the check and drop it, piece by piece, all over his spotless suit.

But, of course, she wouldn't. It galled her to realize that he probably knew what she was thinking, and knew, further, that she was in no position to throw his offer back in his face. He saw the flash of fire, which she fought to control.

"I don't understand, Mr. Pierson. If you're willing to pay all this money, why not just hire a competent sitter?"

"Because I need someone I can trust to oversee the care of my son, Ms. Leary. I can hire all the sitters in the world, but I can't be there to see that they follow my orders. I need to know he's being taken care of the way I want. He's too young to fight for his rights." His voice lowered ominously. "So I do his fighting for him."

Casey heard the thread of danger in his tone. This wasn't a man to be crossed.

"But Danny's not too young to tell me what's going on when I'm not around. Some sitters think a young, healthy boy should spend his entire day in front of a TV. There are a lot of people out there who will simply take my money and run."

"I wish I could help." She started to stand, to signal an end to the conversation. "I'm sure you and Mrs. Pierson can . . ."

"There is no Mrs. Pierson." He bit the words off with venom.

She sank back down in her chair. A three-year-old boy in a strange city, with an ambitious, harassed, and obviously hostile father—and no mother. It was the kind of story that always touched Casey's heart.

"I see." She studied the man across the desk.

The anger glittered brighter in his eyes. There was a

shadow of pain there as well, before he composed himself.

How could she refuse his request? "Have you no relatives . . . ?"

He shook his head wearily.

She took a deep breath. "I'll make out this check for—four hundred dollars." She glanced up quickly to gauge his reaction. Seeing none, she went on. "That will enable me to hire someone immediately. I'll consider this your first month's payment in advance." She rummaged in a drawer and produced some forms. "Please see that these are filled out as thoroughly as possible. They're most important for my files. When would you like Danny to start?"

"Tomorrow." He stood, as if relieved that this interview was concluded. The frown still furrowed his forehead. She had yet to hear a word of thanks from this infuriating, impatient man.

She paused, her hand on the knob. "You said your secretary was Denise Carver?"

He nodded.

She smiled broadly. "I met her when she and her husband first came here. I liked her. Her husband gets out of work nearly an hour before she does, so he always picks up the baby. He's adorable. I love him."

For the first time, Luke Pierson's boyish charm broke through the anger, showing another side of his personality. It was a wicked half-smile that curved his lips but didn't quite reach his eyes.

"The husband or the baby?"

Her eyes rounded in surprise at his impudent question. Then she burst out laughing. "That kind of slip of

the tongue could get me in a lot of trouble, Mr.
Pierson. I'd better watch what I say in the future. I do
love all my children here, but not necessarily their
fathers."

He was pleasantly surprised by her good-natured
acceptance of the joke. As she led the way down the
long hallway to the front door, his gaze trailed her
slender frame in the faded jeans and clinging sweater.
Even from this angle, she was easy to look at. And that
husky laugh of hers was infectious.

A giggling toddler rounded the corner and burst into
her arms with an explosion of energy. Casey scooped
him into her arms and gave him a hug, then settled him
on her hip as she continued walking.

Luke was intrigued. Though she was small, almost
delicate, she exuded energy. And she looked as if she
enjoyed herself. She actually made child care look like
fun.

At the door she paused. "One more thing. We expect
all our children to be picked up in the evening by six at
the latest. Since we start at seven-thirty in the morning,
we have to insist that you be prompt."

He nodded. "Fair enough."

The huge black dog he had spotted earlier lumbered
along the hallway and paused to lick Casey's hand.
Laughing, she opened the door and allowed him to
scamper outside.

"Don't you think he's too big to be allowed inside
with all these children?"

"Trouble?"

"Trouble. What kind of a name is that?"

"It suits him. He's so big and clumsy. When he gets

too happy, his tail knocks over things. Vases, glasses of milk. We have to warn the children to stay out of the way of that dangerous tail, in fact."

"Then why allow him inside? Why not leave him out in this big yard? After all, it's fenced."

She explained as patiently as if he were a child. "Because Trouble is a stray. He apparently came a long distance before settling here. We don't know what he had to go through. We do know he's afraid of storms. Thunder has him cowering under tables. And the dark. If we leave him out after dark, he barks at the shadows. And he's afraid of being left alone. Poor Trouble. He's afraid of just about everything. Except children. He adores children."

He watched her eyes as she spoke. There was a light in them, as if her whole being were lit by some inner radiance.

"And the white cat in there. The one that left its fur all over my leg. Another stray?"

She nodded. "That's Duchess. She lost half her tail in a gate. Patience found her in the back yard."

"Patience?"

"She's one of my assistants. As tough as that old cat. And as loving."

"Kids and old people. Cats and dogs. Is there anything else you shelter here?"

"Patience says I'm a sucker for big, sad eyes." The moment the words were out of her mouth, Casey felt the flush of embarrassment.

"Hmm. I'll have to remember that."

Quickly, she offered him her hand to put an end to

their conversation. "I'll see you and Danny in the morning, Mr. Pierson."

"Luke." He continued to hold her hand for a moment, staring into eyes that suddenly seemed as beguiling as any child's. "Is it Miss or Mrs.?"

"Everyone calls me Casey," she said, evading the obvious question.

His glance darted to the naked ring finger of her left hand, then back up to her eyes. "Casey."

He nodded, then turned away, annoyed with himself. This was a business arrangement, nothing more. The last thing he needed in his already complicated life was a woman, a hard-driving career woman with all those degrees after her name. Especially one with big innocent eyes and glowing cheeks. An odd little thing who took in strays. Who smelled like baby powder. And whose lips looked as soft as rose petals.

He slammed the car door harder than was necessary and turned on the ignition. Now that he had put some distance between them, he could think more clearly. Had he just been conned? The truth was, if she hadn't been so damned determined to refuse him, he probably wouldn't have enrolled Danny in the first place.

He gave another glance at the faded old house. The place and its occupants were a litany of contradictions.

His first impression was right. This wasn't at all what he had expected.

Chapter Two

"What did he want?" Patience Cranston's gaze remained fastened on the infant in her arms, who contentedly finished his bottle. His lids were already closed, sleep just a few moments away.

"He wanted me to make room for his son."

The sharp eyes glanced up, then back to the infant. "And of course you told him there was no room."

Casey shook her head and shoved her hands deep into the pockets of her jeans. "It was a special case, Patience. I didn't have the heart to refuse."

"Uh-huh." The old woman sniffed, then lifted the baby to her shoulder. Staring at Casey, she asked, "And when is there a case that isn't special to you?" Patting the baby gently, she asked, "What is it this time?"

"Hostile man. Obviously hard-driving, ambitious.

And angry at the world, I think. Motherless child. A boy, Danny. Only three years old. Strange new city. No one else to turn to." She shrugged. "That's all I know."

"Why didn't you tell him to hire a baby-sitter?"

"He's already tried a few. It didn't work out."

The older woman smiled gently. "Just pour out your troubles to good old Casey Leary. No problem too big or too small."

"Three years old and no mother. I couldn't say no." Casey's smile grew. "Besides, don't knock it. You know that neighbor of yours who's looking for a job like yours?"

Patience nodded. "Marion?"

"Well, why don't you give me her phone number. I'd like her to come in and interview this afternoon."

"Glory be. You mean this one was a cash customer?"

Casey laughed. Her eyes danced as she shared her secret. "Actually, I asked for more than I needed, hoping to discourage him. But it backfired. He didn't even bat an eye. So," she called as she hurried away, "we get another child, and a chance to employ another senior citizen."

"Hmpf. Senior citizen. Casey Leary, you know how I hate that title."

Casey turned, made a face at her, and hurried back to her office.

It was past six-thirty before Casey deposited the last of her assistants at their senior residence. She had bought the new van to accommodate her elderly employees. It was equipped with a special hydraulic lift to ease their descent to the curb. There were handrails and overhead lights. She was on the road by six-thirty every morning; most of the employees were up before dawn. And after a few weeks of working at the day-care center, all of them admitted that they felt better than they had in years. This job gave them a new lease on life.

"Want to come in for a cup of tea?" Patience invited as the van idled at the curb.

Casey shook her head. "No, thanks. I'm all in." She gave an exaggerated sigh. "Oh, to be eternally young, like someone I know," she said pointedly, "and be able to keep on going from dawn to dusk, with no sign of slowing down."

The older woman was still laughing as she opened the door to her apartment and turned to wave.

On her way home, Casey picked up a sandwich and coffee at a fast-food drive-through. Parking the van, she made her way through the waning spring sunshine to the sprawling house. At the porch, she stopped to examine the first purple crocus that contrasted with the fresh green lawn. By next week, the daffodils, which had just begun to blossom, would be blooming all over the yard. She sighed. Spring in Chicago had always been her favorite time of the year. New flowers, new hope—new life. A knife sliced through her heart, and she struggled to drive away the thoughts that clouded her mind. Why did old pain have to come back to haunt her? When would it ever stop hurting? With fumbling fingers, she unlocked the front door.

As she started to walk inside, the door was caught and held behind her. Startled, she swung around to find Luke Pierson standing there.

"Oh." Her hand went to her throat. Her eyes were wide with surprise. "I—didn't see you."

"Yes. I could tell you were a million miles away. I should have warned you I was here."

His voice seemed softer than it had earlier that day. Less arrogant. Less abrupt. As if he had glimpsed her absorption with her pain and, without knowing why, shared it. His voice, she realized, had a strange effect on her. It slid over her senses like warm honey. Then, just as quickly, it lowered with anger.

"It's dangerous to be so distracted you don't hear someone approaching. You ought to be more careful at this time of day."

Her heartbeat was gradually settling back to its normal rhythm, and she realized that he had voiced her unspoken fear. Putting up a brave front, she said, "I have a big dog inside this house. The minute I screamed, he'd come to my rescue. And there's Vern. He lives in that big old house over there. He's more than my handyman. He's a friend who looks out for me."

"Uh-huh. Well, I don't see either of them at the moment, and by now, you could have been at someone's mercy."

Seeing the look in her eyes, he softened his tone. "I didn't come here to fight with you, Casey. I wanted Danny to see where he would be staying tomorrow. I figured in the morning I'd be too rushed to give him much time to get used to this place before I had to dash off to work."

Now Casey noticed for the first time that there was a young child in the shadows next to Luke. His dark hair was slicked back neatly and his jacket was carefully buttoned. He was a miniature of his father.

"Danny, this is Miss Leary." She heard the emphasis on "Miss" and shot him a glance before turning her attention to his son.

The little boy solemnly offered his hand.

"Hello, Danny. Everyone calls me Casey." She knelt down, eye level, and took his hand.

His eyes were darker than his father's. Brown. And sad. He didn't return her smile.

"Would you like to come inside and see where you'll be staying?"

The little boy looked to his father. "Can we, Dad?"

Luke glanced at the paper bag in Casey's hand. His voice hardened. "I'm afraid we've interrupted Miss Leary's dinner plans."

She grimaced. "Some dinner. I can reheat this. Come on in."

Seeing his son's pleading expression, Luke relented. "All right. But just for a minute."

Although the sunlight still filtered through the large windows, Casey switched on the lights for a brighter effect. Danny's gaze wandered slowly over the toys, now neatly put away for the evening. There were wooden cars and trucks to ride, trains to assemble, and puzzles and card games to improve eye-hand coordination. There were cuddly stuffed animals, and puppets that helped young children talk out their fears and frustrations with the grown-up world.

Slowly, Danny moved about the room, touching this, stroking that, staring openmouthed at a huge stuffed gorilla.

Casey and Luke followed, watching his reaction.

Luke turned slightly to glance at her windblown hair. She seemed fresh, untouched, as casual as a wild daisy in a field.

"In here," Casey called, switching on the light in another room, "is where you can rest, or take a nap." She smiled as he wrinkled his nose. "Don't you take a nap once in a while, Danny?"

"I'm too big for naps," he said proudly. "Naps are for babies. I'm a big boy, right, Dad?"

"That's right, Dan."

Casey smiled. "Most of us here still rest in the afternoon. Even the grandmas who help out."

"Grandmas?" Danny's eyes grew round.

"Didn't your father tell you? We have lots of grand-mas and grandpas here. They'll read to you, or play games with you, or just rock you when you want to be held."

"Just me? And no one else?"

"If that's what you want. But sometimes you'll find out that it's fun to share a grandma with the others."

The little boy turned big, dark eyes to his father. "Did I ever have a grandma, Dad?"

Casey glimpsed a narrowing of the man's eyes.

Luke shook his head. "She died before you were born, Danny."

He thought about this for a while, then began wandering the room once more. "But if I don't want to share her, I don't have to?"

Casey nodded at his grave look. "That's right, Danny." His eyes were so big, so serious. Casey found herself wondering what would put a smile back in them.

Luke glanced at the paper sack Casey was still holding. His tone was abrupt. "Thanks for the tour. Danny and I are on our way to dinner. Let me repay you by taking you with us."

Glancing down at her jeans and sneakers, then at Luke, fresh from the office, she laughed. "No, thanks. I appreciate the offer. But I'm afraid I'm not dressed for dinner, and I'm too tired to go up and change."

"Go up?" He raised an eyebrow.

"I live upstairs," she explained.

"I see. Well, maybe another time." He turned. "Come on, Danny. Say good night to Miss Leary."

The big shaggy dog, hearing the voices, lumbered into the room. The little boy cringed behind his father, peering around his leg with huge, terrified eyes.

"Danny, this is Trouble." Casey knelt down and was immediately knocked over by a large paw planted firmly on her chest.

Before she could scramble up, the dog stood over her, slathering her cheek with his rough tongue.

"No, no. Trouble, get off me." Casey pushed, and the dog dropped to a sitting position. His tail thumped the floor. His tongue continued licking the air.

"Trouble wouldn't hurt a fly," Casey said, brushing her knees and vainly trying to assume an air of dignity. She could feel Luke's gaze burning over her. "His only problem is that he thinks he's a little lapdog. You have to watch out for his tongue. He might lick you to death." Laughing, Casey turned to Danny and realized he was clutching his father's leg in terror.

"I'm not 'fraid," he said, glancing up at his father's stern look. "I just don't like dogs."

"Oh." Casey smiled gently and knelt down beside the trembling boy. "That's too bad. Trouble loves little boys. I think maybe he likes little boys better than anything."

"He does?"

She nodded. "See the way his tail is thumping? That means he's happy. Right now, he's so happy to see you, Danny, that he's laughing. See the way his mouth turns up?"

The little boy stood straighter and studied the shaggy dog. With one hand still clutching his father's leg, he reached out to tentatively touch the smooth fur. His eyes widened. "He's soft."

"He certainly is. Old Trouble has been a pillow to so many children, they go off to find him before they lie down. And this old dog likes nothing better than a nap in front of the fireplace."

"You mean they sleep on him?" The dark eyes grew wider.

"Sort of. They just snuggle down and sink into that soft fur, and pretty soon they're asleep. There is a problem, though."

Danny looked at her.

She smiled. "Trouble snores."

Dark eyebrows raised in disbelief. "Can dogs snore, Dad?"

"I guess, if Miss Leary says so, it must be true."

"Will he snore for me, Casey?"

She laughed. "Trouble doesn't do any tricks on command, Danny. We'll just have to wait until he falls asleep. Then you'll see for yourself."

"Think he'll snore tomorrow?"

"Probably. Some time during the day he's bound to fall asleep."

The dog sprawled on the floor, his head resting between his paws. The little boy took several steps nearer, then reached down and ran his hand over the lush fur. When the dog didn't move, Danny grew bolder. Kneeling down, he ran his hand from Trouble's head to his tail. Immediately, the tail began a rhythmic thumping. Danny backed away before walking proudly to his father.

"I think he likes me, Dad. I can't wait 'til tomorrow. Maybe I'll get to hear him snore."

Cool gray eyes looked over his son's head to meet Casey's nod of approval.

"I'm impressed, Miss Leary. You know your stuff."

The smile lit her eyes. They were, Luke noted, soft green in the artificial light. "That's what you pay me for, Mr. Pierson."

"Let's say our good-byes, Danny."

Danny gave her a solemn look. "Good night, Casey. See you tomorrow. And Trouble, too."

"Good night, Danny." She inclined her head toward the man who stood beside the little boy. "Good night, Luke."

He took her hand and felt the jolt again. A man-woman shock. He had felt it this afternoon and written it off as an automatic response. But now, he was puzzled. It had been a long, tedious day. He was feeling drained. He was preparing his young son for a new life. And still, this strong sexual pull. He didn't like it.

Casey stood in the doorway, still clutching the bag

containing her dinner. She watched as the two figures climbed into the car, one stiff and tense, the other small and afraid. That man, she thought, has an anger inside him big enough to choke on. But beneath his abrupt demeanor, she had glimpsed a tender side, at least where his son was concerned. Although she didn't approve of his heavy-handed methods, she could at least understand what drove him. He loved that little boy and wanted only the best for him.

As Casey locked the door and wandered through the lower rooms shutting off the lights, a big shaggy dog and a white fluffy cat, like shadows of darkness and light, followed her. She found herself thinking about Luke Pierson. She always got personally involved with all her children and their families. It was inevitable. But that stern, angry man had stirred something else in her. She had felt it the moment they met.

Careful, she warned herself as she set the sandwich in the microwave oven and reached for a plate. *You have all the problems you can handle right now. And that man is definitely a problem.*

Cold, she mused as she put on the kettle. Luke Pierson was a cold one. Hostile. Tough. And not above dishing out a little of that anger, she thought. Stay clear of him. He would only bring heartache.

What had taken away their smiles? she wondered. That big, gruff man and that tiny, helpless boy? It had to be the loss of wife and mother. Had she died tragically? Were they forced to stand by and watch, locked in grief? That shared pain would be their bond, even now.

There was so much sadness in the world, Casey reminded herself. Her own problems paled beside the grief and heartache she had heard about from others.

Later, as she passed the mantel on her way upstairs to bed, she ran a hand lovingly over her parents' anniversary clock. Fifty years together. And six children. A legacy of love. She felt tears well up, and she hurried toward the bedroom. She was pushing herself too hard. Whenever she got this tired, she felt close to tears. All she needed was a warm bath and a good night's sleep. And no dreams. Please, she prayed. No dreams tonight. Of warm lips. Of tender touches. Of a faceless lover and a shared future. Just black, silent sleep.

Chapter Three

The sun was barely filtering through the lacy leaves of the red maple when the old house began filling with the sound of children's voices.

The steady tattoo of Vern's hammering on the back porch could be heard above the din. Patience accepted a half-asleep infant from a young mother's arms. Mugs of hot chocolate and plates of toast were set out on the kitchen table for those children who hadn't had time to eat breakfast.

Casey, clad in a plaid shirt and worn jeans, poured the last of the chocolate and hurried along the hall toward the front door.

"Oh. Good morning." She nearly collided with Luke and Danny as Luke threw open the door and walked in. Instantly, Luke reached out to steady her.

His fingers rested firmly on her shoulders. He could

feel the bones through her shirt. She was slender, he realized, almost to the point of being fragile.

She stepped back quickly, alarmed at the way her pulse began racing the minute he touched her. She had known somehow that his hands would be strong.

Danny, dressed in brand-new brown corduroys and a turtleneck sweater of beige and brown stripes, peered around expectantly.

"Where's Trouble?"

With an effort, Casey grinned and pulled her thoughts back from Luke. "Down the hall somewhere. Probably lying under the kitchen table, waiting to catch the crumbs from breakfast. He's a shameless beggar. Would you like some hot chocolate, Danny?"

"Maybe. If Trouble's there." He turned. "'Bye, Dad. See you tonight."

Luke's gaze followed the boy until he was out of sight. There was a frown line between his eyes. "That was easy. I expected . . ."

Casey waited, but he never finished the sentence. What had he expected? Tears? A scene? She wondered if he was relieved or disappointed.

"Did you fill out all the forms I gave you?"

"What?" He seemed distracted.

"The forms. Medical forms, numbers to call in case of emergency."

"Oh. No. I'm afraid I forgot. I'll bring them to you tomorrow."

Her smile disappeared. "Tomorrow could be too late, Luke. I need to know if Danny has any allergies. Has he had all his shots? Who is his doctor? What hospital would I take him to in case of an emergency? These are necessary forms. I can't take the responsibility for him without them."

His temper had a short fuse. "And I said I'd give them to you tomorrow."

"Then you can bring Danny to me tomorrow." She swung around, calling, "Patience, would you bring Danny here, please?"

"Now just a minute."

"No, Mr. Pierson. I don't have a minute. Not for you. I told you I needed those forms. Until I have them, I won't take responsibility for your son. You can bring him back when you have the forms."

His eyes narrowed, and she felt the sting of his anger. For long moments, he stared in silence. Then, expelling his breath, he muttered, "My apartment is all the way over on Lake Shore Drive. I'll have to fight rush-hour traffic."

When she didn't respond, he hissed, "You'll have the forms within half an hour."

"Thank you." She turned away, and he watched as she walked determinedly down the hallway.

Tiny or not, he mused, she walked as proudly as any drill sergeant, holding her head high, her chin jutting at a defiant angle.

Casey could feel his gaze burning into her, but she forced herself to remain calm until she turned the corner.

"Your forms, Miss Leary."

Luke stood on the front porch. Casey held the door

open, but when he didn't make a move to enter, she stepped outside and allowed the door to swing shut behind her.

"Thank you." She held out her hand. Glancing up, she caught the glitter of steel in his eyes. As he handed her the papers, he continued to hold her gaze with a hard, cold look. She softened her tone. "I want you to understand how important all this information is, Luke. Without these forms, I'd be helpless in an emergency. It wouldn't be fair of me to take Danny without the necessary paperwork."

He leaned his hands on either side of her, effectively pinning her against the wall. He brought his head closer, until his face was inches from hers. His voice lowered ominously. "I don't like being backed into a corner. You said I could bring Danny this morning, and then you tried to renege on the deal." His warm breath burned her cheeks, while his words stung her. "Don't ever try that again. You wouldn't want to know how I deal with anyone who double-crosses me."

"I . . ." She licked her lips.

His gaze flicked down, watching the movement of her tongue.

Flustered, she tried to cover her confusion with anger. "I've already explained myself once. I have no intention of doing so again."

"And I have no intention of being pushed around by a skinny little bubblebrain."

"Bubble . . . !" Her eyes widened. He watched the amber shade darken to the color of aged whiskey. "I'm not going to stand here and be insulted. Take your hands off me, you oaf."

There was the slightest pause. "I'm not touching you."

"Then let me go."

"Not just yet."

He knew he was treading on dangerous territory. This wasn't at all what he had intended. But now that they had come this far, he seemed powerless to stop it. Despite his anger, he wanted to taste her lips. And he had the feeling that if he took that step toward her now, she wouldn't stop him. Something sparked between them. He had sensed it the first time he'd met her. And it was there now, ready to burst into flame the moment he touched her.

What would that slender body be like, pressed against his? Would those lips taste fresh, like spring?

Watch it, he cautioned himself. *The last thing you need right now is this woman messing up an already complicated life.*

He stiffened and moved his face back. "I'm sorry. You're right about the forms, of course. And I had no right to call you a bubblebrain."

She took a deep breath and forced herself to speak. "Or skinny."

"You are." His gaze skimmed her figure. "You'd blow away in a good wind. Besides,"—he glowered at her—"you called me an oaf."

"You are. A thickheaded, obstinate . . ."

"Careful." His eyes narrowed.

She took in another breath and swallowed back the angry words that crowded her mind. Gripping the papers tightly, she asked, "Have you filled these out completely?"

"I even dotted all the *i*'s and crossed the *t*'s." Luke dropped his hands and moved back another step. The tension, for the moment, was broken. "I'm late. Tell Danny I'll see him this evening."

She nodded and watched as he swung away and stalked down the steps. For long moments, she didn't move. He had come very close to kissing her. She knew it. And what's more, she hadn't fought it. In fact, she had anticipated what his lips would be like on hers.

"Come on, Danny. As long as your father isn't here yet, you can help me plant my flowers."

Casey cast a sideways glance at the clock and led the little boy outside. Trouble bounded down the steps and rolled in the grass. Duchess made figure eights around Casey's legs, then leaped gracefully to the porch railing, where she curled up in the sunshine.

The porch was abloom with several flats of petunias and impatiens, in rich shades of pink, red, salmon, and purple.

Lifting the first flat, Casey led the way to a flower bed beside the house. The rich dark scent of moist earth carried in the breeze. Vern had been turning and raking the soil all week, in preparation for the planting.

"You take the hand spade and scoop out the dirt like this," Casey instructed, showing Danny how to dig the holes. "Then you take a little plant, set it down inside, and press the dirt firmly around it like this."

"Your hands are all dirty, Casey. Won't your Daddy get mad at you?"

Casey laughed at the innocent question. "When

you're planting flowers, you have to get dirty. It's a rule. Now," she said, digging a second hole, "it's your turn."

Soon she and Danny were working side by side, stopping occasionally to watch the path of a wriggling earthworm, or pausing to watch a parade of ants, some carrying crumbs bigger than themselves.

Before long, the first bed was planted. Casey showed Danny how to gently water the plants, before moving on to the second flower bed.

Luke rounded the corner, then stopped in his tracks. Two slender figures knelt in the dirt. Two heads bent close together, the dark, shiny hair a sharp contrast to the russet, satin sheen. Two voices carried on the air, one a rich, husky laugh, the other a high-pitched note of wonder. Luke's gaze took in the dark, moist earth that clung to shoes, and legs and knees.

"What in the hell . . ."

Casey's head shot up at the sound of Luke's stern voice. Seeing his look, she glanced at Danny. The little boy's knees were caked with mud. Dirt streaked his face and even his hair.

"Making mudpies, Miss Leary?"

She glanced down at her own hands. They were black, the fingernails packed with mud. She was unaware of the trail of dirt that paraded from her forehead to her cheek.

They had avoided another confrontation all week, knowing they struck sparks off each other. Now, hearing Luke's sarcastic tone, her temper flared, but she kept her voice even, mindful of Danny beside her.

"You're late. You know the rules. I expect all the parents to pick up their children no later than six o'clock."

"I instructed my secretary to phone you. She said there was no answer."

Casey realized they'd been outside for over an hour. In the fading sunlight, Luke's face looked haggard. He rubbed his neck wearily.

"Come on, Danny. Let's get you home," he said.

"First we'd better get this dirt off." She studied the mud-soaked knees of the little boy's pants. "That is, if we can."

Taking him by the hand, she led the way through the house to the stairs. The dog and cat were close on their heels. Turning to Luke, she said, "Why don't you come up too. You can fix yourself a drink while I try to repair some of this damage to Danny."

The upper floor of the rambling old house still bore the imprint of a home filled with comfort and good taste. Thick, beige carpeting muffled their footsteps.

Casey called over her shoulder, "The kitchen sitting room is through there. You'll find a bar beside the fireplace. Help yourself." She led Danny to the bathroom, her laughter filling the air. "You and I have some serious scrubbing to do."

Luke glanced around admiringly. Dark hardwood floors gleamed with polish. A Persian rug, in muted shades of turquoise, pink, and yellow on an ivory background, dominated the sitting room. A wall of bookshelves revealed well-worn copies of everything from heavy professional and literary tomes to light fiction and verse. Two white sofas flanked the fieldstone fireplace. The paintings were excellent, several of them old and priceless. One or two contemporary pieces bore famous signatures, including a Calder. A Victorian Valentine stood atop a glass-and-chrome table. Two cane chairs stood on either side of an elegant black lacquer Chinese cabinet. The person who had acquired these had an inquiring mind, far-flung interests.

Every inch of space on the flat surface of the cabinet was taken up with framed photographs. All were family scenes. A giggling Casey, about four or five years old, surrounded by smiling, handsome boys. A grinning Casey, dressed in Easter finery, holding her father's hand. A teenaged Casey, dressed demurely in a bridesmaid's frothy gown and picture hat. Handsome men and pretty wives, surrounded by attractive families, and all bearing a striking resemblance to the woman in the other room. A big, happy, close-knit family.

At the bar, Luke dropped two ice cubes into a crystal glass and poured scotch. Swirling the amber liquid, he walked to the windows. In the fading light of evening, the blossoms of myriad fruit trees shimmered. Their fragrance wafted through the open windows, filling the room with the heady scent of spring.

When Casey didn't smell like baby powder, she smelled of lilacs and apple blossoms. Vibrant, exciting, like spring, Luke thought. With an angry gesture, he loosened his tie. He didn't want to think about Casey again. All week long, ever since he had first met her, she had been flitting into his thoughts, distracting him. Every morning, when he brought Danny to the daycare center, he found himself hoping she'd be at the front door. On days she was there, he left with a light heart. On days when he didn't see her, he found some excuse to stand around at the evening pickup until he spotted her. It was getting out of hand. He had to stop this foolishness.

"Mind fixing me whatever you're having?"

He whirled at the sound of her voice. She was fresh from a shower, wearing a white terry robe. Her feet were bare. She had pinned her hair up, and damp little tendrils trailed her neck and shoulders.

"Scotch all right?"

"Fine."

He fixed the drink and turned to find her standing at the windows, staring down at the yard below. Across the room, Trouble yawned. Duchess curled into a ball on the back of the sofa.

Casey looked up at him. "Danny's playing in the tub. I threw his clothes in the washer. I'm not sure all that mud will come out in one wash."

He shrugged, and he felt the jolt as their fingers touched. What the hell was the matter with him tonight?

"It's okay. They're just play clothes. He'll be back playing in the mud again tomorrow."

He stood beside her and took a long drink. The warmth spread through him and he waited, willing himself to relax. "I got tied up in a meeting this afternoon. I phoned my secretary and asked her to call you. But she got busy with some other calls, and by the time she got around to trying your number, you had left to drive your assistants home. I'm sorry about the mix-up."

She rubbed the back of her neck and sat down on one

of the couches, tucking her feet up under her. "Well, at least Danny learned how to plant flowers. I think he enjoyed it."

"You two looked like you were having a good time." Luke unbuttoned the top button of his shirt and crammed his tie in his pocket. Sitting down on the other sofa, he wearily stretched his legs out and leaned his head back.

He looked so defeated. Casey was shocked at the surge of emotion that almost brought her to her feet. She had an overpowering urge to stroke his temple, to kiss away the lines of fatigue that creased his forehead. Was she getting addled? This man was little more than a stranger. "Did your meeting go well?"

His head snapped up. How long had it been since someone asked him how his day had gone?

She saw the frown on his face. "Was it that bad?"

He chuckled, and Casey realized this was the first time she had ever heard him laugh. She liked the sound of it. It softened his features and lit those gray eyes with warmth.

"No, as a matter of fact, it was a very productive meeting. It went well, Casey."

Their smiles met. They relaxed, for the first time comfortable in each other's presence.

Luke found himself wondering about the slender body beneath the bulky robe. He studied the outline of her high, firm breasts, and felt a rush of heat spreading through him.

"All clean, Dad." Danny rushed into the room, swathed in a thick bath sheet.

"Umm. Now you look like my son. Out there in the

garden, I thought you were somebody else. I said, now who's that stranger playing in the mud with Miss Leary?"

"Aw. You knew me, Dad. Didn't he, Casey?"

She laughed. "I think he's teasing you, Danny. Your father will always know you. After all, you look just like him."

"I do?" Solemn, dark eyes studied the man a moment. "What about my clothes, Casey?"

"Oh." She jumped up. "I'll toss them in the dryer."

When she returned, Casey said, "As long as you two have to wait for the dryer to shut off, why don't I fix something quick for dinner."

"I could send out for something," Luke offered.

"Too much effort. I have some soup simmering on the stove. I'll just make some sandwiches to go with it."

While Casey grilled some ham and cheese, Danny hungrily downed a bowl of vegetable soup and two glasses of milk. Luke searched through the cupboards and managed to set the table. From the bar, he produced a bottle of wine.

"Is white wine appropriate with grilled ham and cheese?"

Casey laughed. "In this kitchen, anything is appropriate, as long as it's edible." She glanced around. "Now where did Danny go?"

Luke left the room and returned a moment later. "He's fast asleep on the floor, snuggled against Trouble. I covered him with your afghan."

"Poor little thing. He's put in a tough day."

"Danny's put in a tough couple of years," Luke

muttered before pulling the cork from the wine bottle with a vengeance.

"It's hard, losing someone you love." Casey felt tears brimming in her eyes and turned away, missing the hard look that crossed Luke's face. When she turned back, with a plate of sandwiches, his features were composed.

"How old was Danny when he lost his mother?"

"Two." Luke didn't like the way this conversation was going. He had no intention of talking about himself. He wanted to keep her at arm's length.

"How did you happen to turn a showplace like this into a day-care center?" Luke held her chair, then moved around the table.

"This was my grandmother's house," Casey explained as she held her glass.

Luke poured the wine, tasted it, then studied the label. "Good. I'll remember to bring you another bottle to replace this one."

"That's not necessary."

He took a bite of his sandwich before asking, "And why are you living in your grandmother's house?"

"After my parents died, I moved in with Gram while I finished college. My brothers are all married and scattered across the country. Gram knew how much I loved this place. So she left it to me."

"How many brothers are there?"

"Five." A dreamy smile crossed her face. "I was the baby. And the only daughter. You can imagine how spoiled I was."

"Ummm." He studied her, recalling the pixie in the photographs, feeling a tightness in his throat. "So your grandmother figured you couldn't take care of yourself, and left you this place. It must take quite a chunk of your income to maintain it."

"You've got it all wrong. She didn't leave it to me because I couldn't fend for myself. She knew how much I loved her home. She and I shared a love for books and art, music, antiques. She knew I would treasure the things she loved, and not just sell them to dealers."

"Like the Matisse."

Casey was surprised and immensely pleased that he shared her knowledge and appreciation of art. "It has the look of a Matisse, doesn't it? It was actually painted by a local artist and friend, Florence Epson. I bought that at her first exhibit, when her work was still unknown. After her death, collectors bought up everything of hers they could find. I could never afford it now," she said lovingly. "I gave that to Gram on her ninety-first birthday. I told her it was time she had something modern. She loved it. Besides, it picked up the colors of her Persian rug."

"I noticed." He noticed, too, the color of her eyes when she was at ease. Pale amber, like cool wine.

"I saw a faded patch on one wall. What happened to the painting that hung there?"

She squared her shoulders and kept the smile in place. "That was another Epson. I needed a van for my employees. It wasn't one of my favorites, and the offer was too good to pass up."

Luke had to admire the way she handled her emotions. It was obvious that everything in this house was special to her. Yet, when she had to, she could be practical.

"But why a day-care center?" he asked.

"I like children."

"Then why not marry and have half a dozen, like your parents? I'm sure there are plenty of men standing in line for your hand."

She froze. The smile faded a fraction as she fought for control.

He had said the wrong thing, though he couldn't imagine what. Then it dawned on him. His tone hardened. "I see. A dedicated career woman. Marriage and children would just be in the way."

She sipped her wine until she felt calm enough to respond. Her throat was so tight she wasn't certain the words would come out. She thought she would choke on them. "Don't knock it. I do provide a service for people like you. You wouldn't be free to pursue—oil leases, isn't it—without a day-care center like mine."

He lifted his glass in a salute. His words were clipped. "Absolutely right. And for that, I thank you."

She took a deep breath and easily changed the subject. "Tell me about your business, Luke. Pierson-Ferris."

He wondered if he only imagined her withdrawal. She was holding a long-stemmed glass, sipping her wine and staring intently at him. Yet, he had the oddest sensation that she had already turned inward.

"We're a small, independent oil company. My father and grandfather started the company in Texas. Now there's just me left in the family. And Danny," he quickly amended. "When I got out of college, I took in my roommate, Jack Ferris, and we started wildcatting. It was a wonderful time in my life. We were two gamblers, out to set the oil world on its ear. We began branching out, looking for new oil deposits. Our latest venture is in the Midwest. There are a lot of oil and gas deposits in Michigan, Indiana, Illinois."

"You must miss Texas."

"Sometimes." What he missed were the years of hard work, of driving ambition, of youthful innocence. When had it all started to crumble? When had he realized that nothing would ever be enough to satisfy Lyn's appetite for status? There had been so many clues, if only he had taken the time to notice. He was sick and tired of his world of high finance, and her world of high fashion. He had a need to get back to his roots.

Luke's mood, Casey noted, became tense when she asked him about his home and company. Maybe the business was faltering. After all, oil speculation was a very shaky business.

"But why uproot yourself and your son? Why not stay in Dallas and leave the Midwest operation to someone else?"

He frowned. It was a question he'd asked himself a million times. He missed his ranch. The home office in Texas needed his expertise. And they could easily afford someone else in this area. But right now, in his turbulent life, he needed this excuse. He had to leave Dallas and its unhappy memories. He needed to turn his back on everything safe and secure and try his hand at something untried, or he'd go crazy. Maybe he was just chasing rainbows, seeking the happier, more carefree existence of his youth.

"Maybe I needed to take a risk."

She shook her head, unable to comprehend. When her world had fallen apart, she had needed this cocoon of safety, this snug, comfortable haven. Gram had understood. That's why she had guaranteed that Casey would have something of her own.

Yet, she had to admit, wildcatting suited Luke. When she had first seen him, she had known he wouldn't be content to be just an executive. He had the look of a rogue, an individualist. Yes, he would be a man to take risks.

"Come on." Luke pushed his chair back and stood. "I'll help you with the dishes. Then I have to get Danny home to bed."

"It would be a shame to wake him now. Why not let him spend the night here? I have a spare bedroom."

His look hardened. "No. Danny's not one of your strays. He's my responsibility. He goes with me." The words were clipped.

"I didn't mean . . ." Casey bit her lip. She had made the offer out of kindness. Yet Luke was right. Danny was his responsibility. Probably his only one. And she'd be darned if she would make it easy for him to shirk his duties, she thought defensively.

They loaded the dishwasher, each uncomfortably aware of the silence that stretched between them.

Casey handed Luke Danny's clothes, warm from the dryer. He dressed the child quickly, deftly, as though he had been doing it a long time. She stood and watched, trying not to involve herself. When one shoe wouldn't go on over the curled toes, she instinctively bent to help. Their heads collided, and Casey felt the knot in her stomach tighten.

"I said I can manage." Luke's tone was curt.

Awkwardly, she stepped back.

Luke finished, then stood and turned to her. "Thanks for dinner and—everything."

"You're welcome."

He bent and lifted the boy in his arms, burrowing him against his big shoulder. Casey held the door. Luke stared down at her a moment. The delicate fragrance of lilac and apple blossom wafted through the open window, surrounding them.

"Maybe you should take my afghan. It'll be cool outside."

As she made a move toward the sofa, he placed his hand on her arm to stop her. She stiffened.

His voice lowered. "Don't bother, Casey. We're fine." His hand moved upward to brush a wisp of hair that drifted across her cheek. "And so are you. You're just fine. Only . . . don't fuss over us. We manage alone just fine."

His touch paralyzed her. For a breathless moment he wound the strand around his finger, staring down into her eyes. With a sigh of impatience, he stepped back, then strode quickly through the open doorway.

Chapter Four

"I can't figure Danny," Patience muttered, settling herself into a chair across from Casey's desk. "Have you noticed that he never smiles?"

Casey frowned, nodding her head. "We've all become aware of it." She bit her lip. "I've seen him laugh a few times, when something really crazy happens. But the smile never stays in his eyes. They're the saddest eyes I've ever seen."

Patience tapped a bony finger on the arm of the chair. "That little guy's been hurt. It's as if he's waiting, almost anticipating getting hurt again."

Casey's eyebrow arched. "I think you're right, Patience. You've just put your finger on the real problem. Danny's afraid to allow himself to get too happy, because he thinks the happiness will be taken away from him again." Her voice lowered. "How tragic that someone so young should be afraid of life's pain."

Patience gave Casey a steady look. "It's tragic at any age."

"And just what are you implying?"

Patience fixed her dark gaze on her young friend. "When are you going to come out of hiding, Casey?"

Casey's throat went dry. "I—I'll talk to Danny's father." Avoiding her friend's probing stare, Casey pushed back her chair and stood. "I've got lunch duty today. Let's see what I can throw together."

Watching her retreating figure, Patience leaned back and expelled a long sigh. Why, she wondered, did intelligent people fail to see the obvious?

With nervous energy, Casey went about her day's routine, trying to block out her friend's mocking words. When the parents began arriving, she was still working at high speed, ready to greet each of them with a special word.

"Darren was listless today," Casey murmured sympathetically to a young mother.

She heard the door open and saw Luke walk in. Avoiding his gaze, she forced herself to concentrate on the young mother and child.

"His temperature was a little on the high side. Of course, with toddlers, that's routine enough. But I think he's coming down with something. Maybe you'd better plan on taking a day or two off from work."

At the woman's sound of protest, Casey smiled gently. "You've earned a few days off. Look how hard you've been working. Besides, see how happy Darren is to see you."

As the baby twined his chubby arms about his mother's neck, she gave Casey a bright smile. "Thanks, Casey. You're right. I think Darren and I will spend all day tomorrow together. Resting."

Seeing Danny across the room, playing quietly with some puppets, Luke leaned against the wall in a careless pose and listened to the conversation.

When the young mother and child left, he crossed his arms over his chest. "Very encouraging. Are you sure you didn't study parent psychology as well?"

Casey grinned. "Child psychology and parent psychology go hand in hand."

He nodded toward the closing door. "Not only will she get a day off work, but she'll get it without a twinge of guilt."

Casey grew serious. "That's the way it should be, Luke. Parents shouldn't be made to feel guilty because their children sometimes have to come first. Employers have to be more compassionate about such situations."

He gave her a mock bow. "Ms. Leary—champion of parents' rights."

Casey gave a quick glance in Danny's direction, then said, in a lower voice, "I'd like to talk to you about Danny."

Instantly his smile faded. "Is he coming down with something too?"

"No." Seeing his look of concern, she added, "My assistants and I are concerned with finding a way to—make him smile."

Luke pushed away from the wall to stand tensely. His words were edged with steel. "Don't try applying your psychology to Danny. Or to me. I pay you to take care of his needs while I work. That's where your responsibility ends, Casey."

"To take care of his needs." Her voice hardened. "Every person needs the warmth of a smile in their life."

Luke moved closer until she could feel the heat of his body. His gray eyes seemed to darken to smoke. His hot breath stung her cheeks. "Back off, Casey." His voice was rough, his temper barely held in check. "Stay out of our lives."

Glancing up, Danny spotted his father. Running to him, he reached up his hands. Luke scooped him into his arms and turned quickly away. Casey stood, her hands on her hips, fuming with impotent anger.

"'Bye, Casey," Danny called over his father's shoulder.

By the time Casey reached the porch, Luke and Danny were in the car. Both heads turned to study her. One small hand lifted in a salute. Two large hands gripped the wheel, as the car roared off in a cloud of dust.

The days flew by in a rush of work. Casey wondered whether Luke was deliberately avoiding her or if their busy schedules prevented them from meeting. By the end of the week, she was determined to try to broach the subject again with Luke. When he arrived to pick up Danny, Casey was waiting.

"I'd like to talk to you about Danny."

Luke had left his suit jacket in the car. His tie was loosened, his shirt rumpled. Running a hand wearily through his hair, he spoke curtly. "Can it wait, Casey? I've put in a long day."

Subdued, she nodded and turned away. She was stunned to feel his hands suddenly grip her shoulders, stopping her in her tracks.

His deep voice, close to her temple, sent ripples along her spine. "I'm sorry. I didn't mean to be so abrupt. It isn't your fault my schedule is so crazy." He turned her until she was facing him. "If you really want to talk about Danny, we could talk over dinner tonight."

As she began to protest, he added, "I need time to feed Danny and get him settled down for the night with a sitter. After that, I promise to give you my undivided attention." His hands remained on her arms. His simple touch warmed her skin. A hint of a smile curled his lips as he watched her battle her indecision.

"All right. But only because I think we need to talk about Danny."

"Of course," he said, the smile growing. "I'll pick you up around eight."

Music from the stereo in the living room filtered into the bedroom. The haunting notes of a tenor saxophone hung in the air for a moment before fading. Casey stepped from the steamy shower, patting her moist skin. She selected her dress and shoes with great care and blew her hair dry until it fell into soft waves about her face and shoulders. She was determined not to think about why she had accepted Luke's offer against her better judgment. This would be a simple dinner with the father of one of her young charges. They would discuss Danny. Nothing more.

If it meant nothing, she chided herself, why was she taking such pains with her appearance? Feeling all thumbs, she smeared her eye makeup, wiped it clean, and started over. When her makeup was complete, she sat on the bed and slid her feet into sheer hose. Slipping into an ecru silk teddy, she pulled on her dress. Pale pink, with narrow straps at the shoulders, it hugged her bosom, then flared in soft pleats to below her knees. She felt delightfully feminine and sexy. With a sigh of exasperation, she stepped out of the dress, tossed it onto the bed, and rummaged through her closet until she found something more suitable.

The emerald silk dress had long, tapered sleeves and a high neck with matching stock tie. Primly tailored, the skirt was narrow, with a tiny slit at each side of the hem. Casey nodded in satisfaction. This was more appropriate. She was, after all, planning to treat this as a business dinner. She slid her feet into simple black pumps. Clasping a double strand of pearls, she added pearl ear studs, picked up a small black bag, and twirled in front of the mirror. There was no time to debate her choice of dress. She hurried downstairs at the sound of the bell.

The tension had been erased from Luke's features. Wearing a dark suit and pale ivory shirt, he was the picture of health. His dark hair still bore the damp traces of a shower.

His gaze skimmed her trim figure, and he noted the sensuous way the silk clung to her curves. The narrow slits at her hemline intrigued him, drawing his gaze to her legs before moving upward to come to rest on her face. Her cheeks were flushed, her eyes glowing. The color of her dress brought out little green flecks around her pupils. After seeing her for weeks in jeans and sweaters, he suddenly became even more conscious of the beautiful woman before him.

"I hope you like Milanese cooking."

"I like any cooking that isn't mine." She laughed, accepting his outstretched hand.

He led her to his car and settled her inside before walking to the driver's side. As he started the ignition, he said, "I've decided that one of the best things about Chicago is the variety of restaurants. Since I've been here, I've tried dozens."

"Don't you ever cook?"

He frowned as he maneuvered the car into traffic. "I'm a pretty good cook. But after a long day at work, the idea of cooking a meal isn't too appealing. Besides, every time I decide to cook, Danny asks for a hot dog. He'd be happy if he could have that every day of his life."

"You're going to have to broaden that boy's outlook," Casey said, laughing.

"I'm not too worried. At least he doesn't want cornflakes three times a day. My mother used to say that's all I ate until I started school."

"It doesn't seem to have hurt you." Casey gave him a sideways glance, then grasped her hands together in her lap. He was close enough to reach out and touch. The thought caused her pulse to race. "My weakness was always peanut butter," she admitted. "Peanut butter and jelly sandwiches. Peanut butter cookies. I'd be a slave for peanut butter fudge."

"Hmmm. I'll have to remember that. It might come in handy if I decide to bribe you." The warmth of his laughter brightened their already light mood.

The restaurant, though large, gave the impression of a small, intimate garden café. Waiters in black suits with white towels draped over their arms cheerfully poured wine and explained the Italian words on the menu.

Casey and Luke sat together on a padded wicker love seat. The table was wrought iron painted white, with a flickering candle in an empty wine bottle. Above them, tiny lights twinkled like the light from a million stars.

Seated here beside Luke, sipping wine, listening to the muted voices above the sound of a mandolin, Casey felt the cares of her life slip away. For a little while, she didn't want to worry about meeting her payroll or about the city inspector who would surely be around in the next few weeks, peering over her shoulder. But common sense warred with her romantic nature, and as always her sense of duty won.

"About Danny," she began as she twirled the last of her pasta on her fork.

Luke's smile faded. "Let it be, Casey."

"But this is why we're together," she insisted. "I agreed to dinner only because you said we could talk."

"And I thought it was my magnetic personality." He sighed. "All right. Talk." Picking up his glass of wine, he leaned back.

"Patience feels that Danny has been so hurt by the

loss of his mother that he's afraid to enjoy anything too much for fear of losing it. She said it's as if he's anticipating being hurt." Casey studied Luke's face. It was hard, but composed. A mask, showing no feeling.

"Do you agree with Patience?" he asked.

She nodded. "I've seen Danny laugh with the other children. But the laughter doesn't linger in his eyes. I think he's afraid, Luke."

"Of course he's afraid." Luke's grip tightened on the stem of his glass until, realizing what he was doing, he set it down quickly. "He has a right to be afraid. There aren't any guarantees in this life, Casey. You know that."

"But he's so young to be so badly disillusioned. Children should be free to rush headlong into life, trying everything, tasting all of it."

He smiled at her fervor. "Is that what little Casey Leary did?"

She grinned, and Luke watched the color flood her cheeks.

"Yes. With five older brothers, I always seemed to be rushing to keep up. I had no chance to be a delicate, helpless little girl. The only time my mother ever got me into a dress was for church or very special occasions." Her eyes crinkled with laughter at the memories. "I climbed every apple tree in the neighborhood. I tormented the neighbors' dogs. Every time someone got into mischief, I was a part of it. My poor parents. They despaired of ever having a dainty, feminine daughter."

The thought of the delicate, beautiful woman beside him as a young tomboy caused him to smile before he said, "Not every child is lucky enough to be born into a home filled with love and laughter, Casey. Danny doesn't have a loving mother or brothers and sisters to fill the void. He only has me." His voice dropped to nearly a whisper. "And I'm afraid I'm not always up to the task. I'm gone most of the day."

She touched his arm. "I'm not trying to lay any guilt on you, Luke. Please don't blame yourself. Danny's a wonderful little boy. You're doing a fine job."

"But . . ." He watched her eyes.

"But, I'd like to see him smile."

"So would I." His gaze seemed so distant that for a moment Casey felt he was unaware of her presence.

He turned. "What makes you keep on wanting to taste life, Casey?"

"What?" She shrank back from his direct stare. "What do you mean by that?"

"The people you reach out to. The strays. It seems almost a contradiction that at the same time you're reaching out to people, you back away from life and hole up in your grandmother's house."

"That's . . ." She licked her lips. ". . . not true. I'm having a wonderful time with my friends and my day-care center. And besides, my life is none of your business."

He noted the way she lifted her chin, denying his words. His voice grew toneless. "You're right." He signaled the waiter. "Coffee and dessert?"

She nodded, relieved that he had so easily changed the subject. "I never pass up dessert."

He glanced at her and saw the stiff way she gripped her hands, and the lines of tension around her mouth.

He had touched a nerve. But he still didn't know anything more about her than before. She was a mystery. Just as he was to her. Maybe it would be best to keep it that way.

Luke handed the parking attendant the ticket for his car. The night had grown cool. He put his arm about Casey's shoulders and felt her shiver.

"Here." He slipped off his suit jacket and draped it over her. His fingers brushed the back of her neck, sending little tremors rippling through her. The mere touch of him was enough to make her tingle.

"Thanks." She smiled up at him, and saw a flicker of something in his eyes.

They got into the car, and Luke turned on the radio. Violins formed a tender background. A singer crooned a haunting ballad of lost love. Luke held a lighter to his cigarette, then snapped it shut, leaving them in darkness. As he drove, both of them seemed content to be silent.

Luke's voice was the first to break the spell. "Tell me more about your childhood, Casey. Did you grow up here in Chicago?"

"Uh-huh. Just a few miles from Gram's house. I used to boast that I'd see the whole world before I settled down." She laughed. "And here I am, still in Chicago, living in the house where my mother grew up. I didn't get very far, did I?"

His voice in the darkness was deep, thoughtful. "I don't think it matters how far we travel. We still end up having to live with ourselves, our successes or failures. Ultimately, I suppose, we have to take a few risks in order to achieve anything." He stubbed out the cigarette in the ashtray. Then he reached over and caught her hand. "I'm glad you insisted on talking to me about Danny tonight. You're right, of course. I've been evading the obvious. He's afraid of getting hurt. Maybe he's even afraid I'll leave him too. Then he'd be completely alone."

"Does he talk about it?"

Casey felt his hand squeeze her fingers before he responded. "No. And I haven't encouraged him. I've been too wrapped up in my own problems. But I'll get him to start talking to me about his fears."

"Good."

Luke drove along the curving driveway of her old house, then stopped the car and turned to her. "I guess I've been so busy taking risks in my business, I've forgotten how to take risks in my personal life." His voice sounded strained. "But once burned . . ."

Her breath caught in her throat. Realizing that an awkward silence had stretched between them, she murmured, "I have to go in now, Luke."

"I thought we'd talk." His voice lowered.

Casey felt a thread of alarm. "About what?"

"Danny. Life. Your favorite color. Whether the moon is really made of green cheese. Peanut butter. You. Me."

She could learn to love the deep, rich voice, the warmth of his chuckle. "No." The darkness of the car was too unsettling. Or maybe it was the nearness of this man. "I haven't the time, Luke." She opened the car door and hurried up the steps. At the top of the stairs, Luke's hand clutched her shoulder. She spun to face him.

"So this is what happened to the little girl who was always rushing through life—who was always into mischief. She's still rushing."

"Yes. But she grew up. She had to learn to become sensible." Casey backed up a step until she felt the coolness of the stone wall against her back. "Good night, Luke. Thank you for the lovely dinner."

"You're forgetting something."

Her eyes widened. "What?"

"My jacket. Or did you want to wear it to bed?"

"Oh." She heard the warmth of his laughter, and joined him. As she began to remove the jacket, he caught her by the lapels, pulling her closer.

He inhaled the delicate fragrance of lilac and apple blossom that surrounded them. He wasn't certain whether it came from the air around them or the woman in his arms. He hadn't wanted this, hadn't wanted any more complications in his life right now. Yet the perfumed night and this woman conspired to defeat all his good intentions.

Beneath the lapels, he could feel the soft swell of her breasts. His heartbeat quickened. He wanted to feel her in his arms. He needed to hold her. He had to taste her. He ached to explore her body. He bent his head down. The moment his lips touched hers, the world exploded in a flash of lights. His breath mingled with hers, a sudden hot burst as he reacted to the shocking sensations.

He hadn't intended to kiss her. In fact, he had studiously avoided it. But now, as the kiss grew, as his lips moved over hers, he became caught up in feelings too strong to ignore. All his good intentions fled. Her silken hair brushed his hands, and he reached up, twining his fingers through the strands.

Shocked at the depth of feeling he experienced at the simple touch of her, he lifted his head to study her. Her confusion was apparent in her wide, luminous eyes. Her mouth rounded in a sigh.

Ever so slowly, he drew her to him again, watching her eyes. They widened in surprise, then the lids fluttered down, anticipating another kiss.

"Casey. Open your eyes."

Her lids fluttered. "Why?"

"Because I want to see me in them. I want you to see yourself in mine."

She stared into his eyes, feeling a hypnotic pull. She had feared this. But now, suddenly, seeing herself reflected in those smokey eyes, she wanted desperately to taste his lips again. Her breath seemed to die in her throat. Even her heartbeat seemed stilled, waiting, watching.

He lifted a finger to her lips, tracing their fullness, feeling their velvety warmth. He lowered his head until his lips hovered above hers.

Then his lips covered hers again, sending a spasm of shock waves through her. His arms came around her, enfolding her, crushing her to him.

He had known that she tasted like springtime, like cool water. He knew her lips were like the tender petals of a rose. What he hadn't expected was this wild, primitive response. His heart was pounding out of control. He had intended only to taste his lips, to kiss her, then walk away. But he couldn't settle for one taste. He wanted it all.

She had been so reluctant to kiss him. But now, her mouth moved on his, igniting him. Her hands slid to his chest and felt the drumming of his heartbeat. It was as thunderous as her own. Sliding her hands around his waist, she clung to him, needing his strength.

His hands suddenly gripped her shoulders, holding her a little away from him. His eyes narrowed as he studied her. For long moments he stared into wide, amber eyes, as though searching for answers to his unspoken questions. Then, almost roughly, he pulled her toward him and brought his lips down hard on hers.

There was an urgency in the way he kissed her. Casey had never felt such desperation in a kiss. And never before had she responded like this. She had always been careful about giving her love, because she knew she was a person who would love intensely. This man, this angry, hostile, distant man, stirred something in her. He frightened her, yet excited her. And his simple touch unleashed feelings that deeply disturbed her.

Rough hands twined through her hair, drawing her head back. His lips traced her eyebrow, her cheek, her jaw, then returned to cover her lips. His kiss drained her, yet she wanted to give more.

Then, as suddenly as it had begun, the kiss ended abruptly. Clutching her shoulders, he drew her firmly away, and stared for a long moment into her eyes. He could read her confusion, her fear. And something more. The stirrings of passion were evident on her expressive face.

"I'll take my jacket now."

Avoiding his eyes, Casey slid the jacket from her shoulders and handed it to him. She watched him walk down the steps, unable to think of a single thing to say.

He lifted the jacket to his face. It still bore the traces of the delicate scent of her. Turning back, he looked at her for a long time. Then, with a growl of anger, he added, "Still no sign of that trusted watchdog or your neighboring handyman. Bolt your door, Casey Leary. It isn't safe for someone like you to be alone after dark."

Chapter Five

Luke caught his young son's hand and walked up the steps to the day-care center. He was feeling the effects of a sleepless night. Until dawn, he had paced the living room of his penthouse apartment, staring at the lights of the city. His throat was raw from too many cigarettes.

Patience looked up as they entered. Luke's gaze swept the room until he spotted Casey's slender figure on the far side. Bending, she hugged a giggling toddler, then straightened. She hadn't seen him yet, and he allowed himself the luxury of openly staring at her.

From the back of the house a stocky man with a shock of white hair framing a ruddy face hurried toward her carrying an armload of flowers.

"Vern! Lilacs!" She buried her face in the purple mass; then threw her free arm around his neck, giving him a great bear hug. "Oh, you dear. How I love them."

"I knew they were your favorites, Casey. Got lots more in my yard. I'll pick some more in a few days."

"I have to find a vase. Oh, Vern, thank you." She hugged him once more before rushing off toward the kitchen.

Luke felt an insane jealousy toward the old man. His simple, kind gesture had brought Casey such pleasure. And freely, without restrictions, she had hugged him. She was that way with everyone. She could pick up a child, swing him to her hip, and make him feel loved without any seeming effort on her part.

Luke glanced around at the smiling, lined faces of her assistants, and he saw Patience's dark gaze studying him. He flushed uncomfortably and turned away. Casey was constantly touching, hugging, patting, making all of them feel cared for.

Except with him. She held back, stiff, awkward, when she was with him. But last night he had felt her response to his touch. Beneath the cheerful good humor, hidden behind the waiflike casualness, was a slumbering passion.

"'Bye, Dad. I want to go find Trouble."

Luke lifted his son to eye level and smiled. "I think you and Trouble are becoming buddies."

"Yep." The solemn eyes were unblinking.

"Okay, Danny. See you tonight." Luke kissed his son and set him down. Then, without taking time to think it through, he turned away from the door and headed toward the rear of the house.

Casey was arranging the mass of lilacs in a black ice

bucket. Smiling, she turned at the sound of footsteps. "Hi." Color flooded her cheeks at the sight of him. "Look what Vern brought me."

He stopped beside her, inhaling the delicate fragrance. "So that's the brave handyman who's going to protect you?"

She shot him a look. "He's very strong."

"Oh, I could tell. Underneath the lilacs his muscles were bulging."

She laughed and broke off a sprig. "Here, tough guy. You could use some softening influences yourself. When you feel like taking your secretary's head off today, stop and smell the flowers instead." She pulled the stem through the buttonhole of his suit jacket and smoothed his lapel.

Stopping her hand, he continued to hold it as he stared down at her. "How do you spend your weekends?"

"The same as everyone else. Laundry. Chores. Shopping. Why?"

"I promised Danny I'd take him to see one of our sites. Since it's far from the city, I thought it might be fun to make it a picnic. How about joining us?"

"Well, I . . ." She tried to remove her hand from his grasp, but he tightened his grip.

"He's crazy about Trouble. I thought we could bring him along too. And Duchess, if you'd like."

"Duchess hates cars."

Luke's mind was racing. He wasn't going to let her get away now. "With you and Trouble along, I think I might get Danny to open up a little. And you're good at bringing him out of his shell."

She bit her lip. "I suppose for Danny's sake. . . ."

"Great. We'll pick you up early. Around nine."

She laughed, and Luke found himself enjoying the husky tone of her laughter. "It sounds like fun. And Trouble will love a romp in the country. What'll I bring?"

"Nothing. I'll take care of everything." He reached over and tucked a strand of her hair behind her ear. For a brief moment, their gazes locked. Then she swung away with the vase of flowers in her hands.

He touched the sprig of lilacs at his lapel, then hurried off to work, surprised, yet pleased with himself. It had been a pretty cheap trick, using Danny's problems to coax her along. But it had worked.

So much for good intentions. Some time in the early hours of the morning, he had come to the conclusion that his life was messed up enough without any further complications. Then, the minute he saw her, all his resolutions were forgotten. He knew he had to be with her again. But it was only a harmless day in the country, he consoled himself. And they would be well chaperoned, with Danny and Trouble along.

The curtains of Casey's bedroom billowed inward on a gentle breeze. Duchess yawned, then curled herself contentedly on the neatly made bed. Trouble, fresh from an early-morning inspection of the yard, circled several times, then settled down in a patch of sunlight.

Casey pulled on a pair of white cotton slacks and tied a bright apricot shirt at her midriff, exposing a brief expanse of pale skin. Tying her hair back with a bright ribbon, she left her face free of makeup, adding only a touch of gloss to her lips. Slipping her feet into comfortable sandals, she picked up a white cotton sweater and headed downstairs at the sound of the doorbell. Trouble bounded ahead of her, barking his warning at the approaching visitors.

When she threw open the door, Trouble's tail thumped a welcome at the little boy who stood waiting on the porch.

"Casey, we're going on a picnic."

"Yes. Isn't this fun?" She smiled at Danny's eager expression. Dressed in dark shorts and a T-shirt, he had left his sneakers untied in his impatience.

"Here," she said, kneeling down. "Give me your foot."

Quickly, she tied the laces into neat bows.

"Good morning. Ready?" said Luke.

Casey stood and felt the familiar jolt of Luke's presence, then forced herself to smile up at him. She had always seen him wearing perfectly tailored business suits. Today, dressed in trim-fitting jeans and a cotton shirt, with the sleeves rolled above his elbows, he looked even more like a rogue.

The little boy and the shaggy dog ran ahead of them toward the car and scrambled into the back seat.

So this was the morning she had dreamed of all night. Why was she so bothered by the thought of spending an entire day with Luke Pierson? Why did this man disturb her so? Just being near him caused a little tingling sensation at the base of her spine.

"I hope you haven't had breakfast," he said as he started the car.

"Just coffee. Why?"

"Because I promised Danny we'd stop for an egg and sausage patty on a bun. Believe it or not, he thinks that's a better breakfast than homemade."

"My kind of boy," Casey said, winking at Danny. "That happens to be my favorite breakfast too."

"Ugh. I can see I'm going to have to educate both of you. My mother used to turn out a Sunday breakfast of potatoes, homemade sausage, and scrambled eggs that I would die for."

"What happened to the boy who ate cornflakes?" Casey asked innocently.

"He grew up and discovered what real food was."

"Personally, anything that's cooked by someone else is real food to me." Casey laughed.

They drove to a fast-food restaurant, where Casey and Danny ordered their favorite breakfast while Luke settled for coffee.

Fortified, they drove through the city, the streets free of the usual work-week traffic. The warm spring sunshine had brought out dozens of joggers, moving in their steady rhythm beneath towering office buildings.

Gradually the blocks of commercial buildings gave way to apartments and condominiums, and then to suburbs, with graceful houses and manicured lawns, neighborhood schools and churches, and playgrounds with children squealing as they flashed down slides or pumped high on swings.

"Where are we headed, Luke?"

He turned to her, enjoying the way the sunlight streaming through the car window surrounded her like a halo.

"I've taken an option on a tract of land in the country. We'll start drilling next week. It's always a gamble, of course. But if there's oil, it's worth it."

"And if there isn't?" she asked.

He shrugged. "That's the chance I take."

"How many times can you afford to be wrong?"

"The oil business was built on speculation. We can't afford to stop taking risks."

She studied his strong profile. "But each time you make a wrong guess, doesn't it get harder to keep on taking a chance?"

He turned his head. Seeing the doubt in her eyes, he held her gaze with a steady look. "Yes, Casey. The fear of failure is what keeps so many people from succeeding. But I know now that the only way to hold that fear at bay is to force myself to risk it all again."

"Even if someone gets hurt?"

He glanced at her hands, clutched tightly in her lap. "Yes. Even if someone gets hurt. No guarantees. Remember?"

She was grateful when Luke turned his attention to driving the car onto a single dirt road, lined with a tangle of trees and growth that signaled the beginning of the property they would inspect.

"Are there any bears out here, Dad?" Danny's voice was edged with anticipation.

"Sorry, not a one. But we might see a deer, or a rabbit."

"Oh, boy. Come on, Trouble."

Danny bounded from the parked car and ran to the top of a hill, the dog trailing beside him.

"It's odd," Casey said, slipping out of the car and looking around. "I'd never expect to see oil in such a tranquil setting."

Luke caught her hand, then lifted it for his inspection. It seemed so small in his. "Looks are deceiving. Nothing is ever as it seems." With a grin, he twined his fingers in hers and said, "Come on. Danny's got the right idea. We can see the whole site from the top of that hill."

While they walked, Danny and Trouble bounded ahead, scaring up pheasants whose wild whirl of wings and excited squawks left the two of them frozen in midstride, watching the spectacle.

At the top of the hill, Luke pointed. "Down there, beyond that fringe of bushes, is where we took the soil samples. They'll start the drilling there."

"It must be exciting, watching them drill for oil. Will you be here every day?"

"I'd like to come, but there are other claims on my time. Danny, for one. This is a long way from Chicago. And there are other parcels of land to inspect. We always have to have something in reserve, in case this land doesn't yield what we'd hoped for."

The wind at the top of the hill swirled about them, whipping her hair about her face. Hearing Luke's words, Casey began to feel a sense of the excitement that drove him. What a thrill it would be if they actually found oil on this property.

Suddenly, the stillness was interrupted by the sound of Trouble barking frantically. Then they heard Danny's voice.

"Dad! Casey! Come here. Hurry!"

His shouts sent them flying down the hill toward a stand of trees. Still barking, Trouble leaped at the base of a tall tree.

Danny pointed. "Look, Dad. Up there."

Perched on a high branch, peering at them through the dense leaves, was a masked, furry face.

"He was walking over there when Trouble spotted him. Then he ran up the tree. What is he, Dad?"

"It's a raccoon, Danny. And a pretty unhappy one right now. Probably not used to seeing big, noisy dogs and little boys in this secluded setting."

"Will he come down?"

"Not until we leave. And certainly not as long as Trouble keeps barking at him. I don't think this old dog will give up for a long time." Luke turned to Casey. "Can you think of a way to coax him away from this tree?"

"Food." She laughed. "That's his greatest weakness."

"Come on, Danny. We'll open a can of dog food and put it where Trouble can smell it. Maybe he can be persuaded to leave the poor raccoon alone for a little while."

As they walked back to the car, the dog sat down at the base of the tree, prepared for a long vigil. But before very long, the familiar scent of mealtime lured him away, and Trouble, as predicted, headed for his food. The three of them shared a smile at Trouble's obvious appreciation of his lunch. Then Luke spoke.

"There's a lake on the far side of these woods. Want to explore it?"

Casey and Danny nodded in unison.

While they walked, Luke dropped his arm about Casey's shoulders. For a moment, she stiffened. But while he chatted comfortably with his son, she realized how much she liked this feeling of closeness. It was something she had always had in her life. And now, she knew that it was something she had been lacking.

At the shore of the lake, Luke instructed Danny to sit while he removed his shoes and rolled his pants to his knees. Following their lead, Casey slipped off her sandals and rolled the cuffs of her white pants. Walking along the water's edge, they collected shells and skimmed stones in the water. Luke showed off for his son, skipping a stone four times before it sank.

"Bet I can beat you," Casey challenged. Picking up a stone, she skimmed it lightly across the waves. It skipped four, then five times before sinking.

"Casey. How'd you learn that?" Danny asked in awe.

"I had five older brothers," she said, laughing. "And for years they could beat me at everything. It took me a long time to catch up. But once I did, I was unbeatable."

Luke gave her an admiring glance. "All right. Let's have a contest. Loser has to clean up after dinner."

"You're on."

"One stone. One chance."

"I'm betting on my dad," Danny said proudly.

"Then you'll get to clean up with him," Casey teased, picking up a stone.

"Ladies first." Luke made a sweeping gesture with his hand.

Casey skimmed the stone. It skipped four, five, and narrowly missed a sixth time before plopping below the waves. She turned to Luke. "Give it your best shot, sir."

Turning sideways, he tossed the stone, watching it skim the waves. It skipped six times before plunking into the water, leaving widening circles to mark the spot.

"I don't believe it," Casey said, enjoying the look of pride on Danny's face. "I think your father set me up."

"Well, you gave it a good try," Luke said nonchalantly. "It just wasn't good enough."

"I should know better than to gamble with a gambler," she muttered.

"Danny," Luke said expansively, enjoying his son's happy grin, "I think our picnic is going to be even more enjoyable, knowing we don't have to clean up afterward."

With a squeal of laughter, Danny and Trouble ran off in search of more stones to toss.

Catching a lock of Casey's hair that blew across her cheek, he smiled down into her upturned face. "But if you're nice to me today, I could be persuaded to help you."

"A deal's a deal. I'll pay up."

He wound the strand of hair about his finger, drawing her face closer. "We could find some other form of payment." His lips were a breath away. Still, he didn't kiss her, but merely watched as the amber color of her eyes deepened. Her lids fluttered invitingly, and still he hesitated.

She wanted the touch of his lips on hers, needed to see if the explosion of feelings he had ignited before would be there again. She forgot the fear, the hesitation. The wall that she had kept so carefully around herself was crumbling. At last, unable to bear even the smallest distance between them, she lifted on tiptoe to brush his lips with hers.

She felt his slight intake of breath as their lips met. Still, he didn't hold her; he merely kept his hand entwined in her hair. The other hand was clutched rigidly at his side.

Casey grew impatient for his touch. The kiss wasn't enough. She wanted to feel the passion she had sensed that first time. She needed to test the careful control he seemed to keep over his emotions.

She slipped her arms around his waist and drew him near. His low moan of pleasure thrilled her as she deepened the kiss. She felt his fingers tighten on her hair, then slid to the back of her head, changing the angle of their kiss. Still he kept his other hand at his side.

She drew back, watching him. His eyes narrowed slightly. As she started to turn away, he caught her shoulders.

"Was it there?" His voice was low, barely a whisper.

"What?"

"Whatever it was you were looking for."

"No."

"Oh, it's there. You just didn't look far enough. Care to try again?"

She knew she should walk away. She should shout no at the top of her lungs and run, before it was too late. But it was already too late. The mere touch of his hands on her shoulders was her undoing.

She melted against him and raised her lips to his. Now his kiss was no longer passive. Hot, hungry, his mouth moved over hers. He took the kiss deeper, drawing her with him into a passion that left them both aching. For so long, he had tried to deny his need. Now, unleashed, a kind of madness took over his control.

All his thoughts centered on the woman in his arms. Her breasts were flattened against his chest. Her breath mingled with his, coming in quick bursts as she returned the kiss.

His hand found the bare expanse of her skin beneath the tied shirt, and his fingertips moved upward, whispering over her breast. For a moment she stiffened in resistance. His touch was gentle, seductive. No one had ever awakened such feelings in her before. She could taste the hunger in his kiss, and it fueled her own hunger.

"Oh God, Casey, how I want you."

She struggled against the seductive words. She needed to fight her way back to reality. The overpowering need for him was clouding her senses. "This can't be right. What are we thinking of? In the middle of the day, with Danny . . ."

"Oh." He ran his hands along her cheeks, then plunged both hands deeply into her tousled hair. "You want moonlight and the cover of darkness for our lovemaking?"

"No. I meant . . ."

Running his finger along her cheek, he smiled down at her confusion. "It's all right, Casey. I know what you mean. And you know what I mean." His voice lowered to a caress. "I mean to have you."

"You tricked me. You let me think I was coming with you today to help Danny."

"And you are helping him. Look at him," he said, glancing in the direction of his son. "He hasn't had such a carefree day in ages. Besides, you needed an excuse to come along with me."

"I did not."

"Good. Then the next time I ask you out, we won't have to resort to tricks. You'll know that I'm asking you because I want to be with you."

"And I can refuse, because I don't want to be with you."

"That's a lie, Casey. You didn't start all this just now because you didn't like me."

She glanced down in embarrassment. He caught her chin and lifted her face for his inspection. Color flooded her cheeks.

"I want you, Casey. And you want me. It's that simple."

"Nothing is ever that simple, Luke. And just because I kissed you, don't think I'll let it go any further."

"Why?" His eyes narrowed as he studied her.

"Haven't you learned by now that you can't have everything you want?" She twisted roughly from his arms.

He issued a low growl of challenge. "I said I want you, Casey. And I mean to have you."

Chapter Six

"Look, Dad. We got too close to the water."

Danny's high-pitched complaint distracted Luke and Casey. They both began laughing at the sight of the little boy, his clothes clinging to him, his hair dripping beads of water down his rosy cheeks. Behind him, Trouble shook himself, sending a spray in all directions.

"Are you sure you didn't jump in?" Luke lifted his son high in his arms, allowing the water to spill down his muscular arms and onto his upturned face.

"No, Dad. A wave came up and caught us."

"I forgot to bring a spare set of clothing," Luke grumbled, setting Danny down on dry land.

"I brought a sweater," Casey said. "Why not wrap him in that, and hang his clothes on some branches. In this sunlight, they should dry in no time."

"Good idea." Luke began removing the wet clothes while Casey hurried back to the car.

In a little while, Danny and Trouble were once more exploring the shore. Casey's white cotton sweater fell to the little boy's ankles. The sleeves were rolled above his elbows. With the big dog for company, Danny didn't seem to mind the inconvenience.

"I don't know about you," Luke said, "but I'm feeling the first pangs of hunger. How about that picnic?"

"Where will we eat?"

Luke pointed. "I spotted a pretty little cove around that bend. Let's take a look." He grabbed Casey's hand, and together they ran along the beach, keeping Danny in sight.

White sand glinted in the brilliant sunlight. Waves lapped gently at the shore. To one side the ground rose toward the hills beyond. Hardy spruce and popular saplings clung to the side of the hill and grew right down to the water's edge. Beneath the trees, sweet clover formed a green-and-purple-hued oasis.

"Oh, Luke, it's perfect."

"So are you." He stared down at her for long, silent moments. Casey felt her cheeks flame. Running his index finger along her cheek, he lifted her chin and dropped a quick kiss on her lips. "You keep an eye on Danny. I'll get the food."

As he walked away, Casey stood transfixed, watching his retreating back. *Careful,* she warned herself. *You're getting in over your head.* But Luke was warm, vital, and exciting. And she had been living a sheltered existence for too long. With a light step, she ran to join Danny and Trouble.

"Can you make Trouble chase a stick?" Danny asked her.

"Any worthwhile dog knows how to fetch," she declared. "Watch."

Picking up a piece of driftwood, Casey held it up. Eagerly, Trouble danced around her, waiting for the stick to leave her hands. The moment she tossed it, he was off like a shot. Leaping in the air, he caught it in his mouth before it hit the ground.

"Wow! What a neat trick!" Danny exclaimed.

Casey laughed at Danny's look of surprise. "You mean you didn't know all the wonderful things he can do? Come on, Trouble, let's show off."

Luke stood at the top of the hill, the picnic basket in his hand, a blanket folded over his arm, and watched the figures below.

"Come on, Trouble. Give me back the stick," Casey coaxed as she pried the driftwood free of the big dog's mouth. "He knows how to fetch. The only problem is, he never wants to give anything back." Handing the stick to Danny, she instructed, "Now, hold the stick high over your head, until Trouble is ready to run. Then toss it as far as you can. He'll catch it before it drops."

As she was showing Danny, the big dog became impatient. Dancing around them, he leaped, knocking them both to the ground. As they tumbled, he took hold of the driftwood with his teeth and ran away. Casey and Danny fell backwards, landing in the wet sand.

Luke laughed so hard at the sight that he had tears in his eyes. After sauntering down the slope, he stood over them as they brushed sand from the seats of their pants.

"Hey, that was a great trick. Know any more?"

Casey assumed an air of wounded dignity. "He just gets a bit overanxious."

"Overanxious! That clumsy animal is about as graceful as an elephant."

"Elephants are very graceful animals," Casey said, ignoring Luke and speaking to Danny. "Have you ever seen them in the circus, parading around the tent or balancing in the center ring?"

"Uh-Uh. I've never been to a circus, have I, Dad?"

Casey's eyes widened. "You've never been to a circus?"

He shook his head. "Nope. What's it like?"

"Well," she said, kneeling in front of him, "there are clowns and tightrope walkers and people who fly through the air. I can see that your father has been very lax in your education. Every little boy should see a circus. Whenever it comes to town, I'll have to remind your father to take you."

"Will you come too, Casey?"

She stared at his happy expression and felt her heart melting. "If you want me to."

"Come on," Luke called, leading the way. "I was up all morning preparing this food."

On the carpet of clover, he spread a blanket. From the huge wicker hamper he removed a bottle of wine and a thermos of lemonade. He set out cold lobster and crab legs from a covered container.

"Ooh," Casey murmured, taking a bite. "Heavenly."

"There's more." Luke uncovered a plate with deviled eggs and a basket filled with flaky rolls.

The fresh air and sunshine, combined with the exertion of walking up and down hill, had made them ravenous. Amid silly conversation, they savored the wonderful meal.

For dessert there were delicate pastries and a bowl of pears and brie.

"I thought I heard you say you prepared this food," said Casey. Over her wineglass, she glanced at Luke and saw a disarming grin spread across his face.

"Well, at least some of it," he hedged.

"Uh-huh. The pears maybe. I'd say the rest of this came from a very fancy restaurant."

She saw the look that passed from father to son. Danny broke into a fit of giggles.

"She caught you, Dad."

"All right. I'll confess. I asked the chef at one of our favorite restaurants to prepare a picnic basket. But I did pick up the pears at a local fruit market."

"How talented of you, Mr. Pierson," Casey said in her most haughty tone. She winked at Luke as Danny broke into another gale of laughter.

"But you believed him for a while, didn't you, Casey?"

"For a few minutes. But somehow, I think if your father prepared this meal, it would have been sandwiches and cookies."

"As long as they're chocolate chip, I wouldn't mind," Danny said.

"Or peanut butter," Luke added, smiling at Casey. Reaching over, he tucked a stray strand of hair behind her ear, then allowed his fingertip to remain at her neck. Casey felt her breath catch in her throat.

"Are you going to kiss my dad?" Danny asked solemnly.

"What kind of question is that?" Casey stiffened.

"I saw you kissing him before, on the beach." Danny reached for a pear and began eating, missing the rush of color that flooded Casey's cheeks.

Luke caught her hand and lifted it to his lips. "My son is very observant." Without shifting his gaze from her face, he asked, "And what do you think about Casey kissing me, Danny?"

"It's okay, I guess. She kisses me sometimes. It's nice. Can I go feed the birds, Dad?"

"Sure, Danny. As long as you don't wander too far."

As the little boy hurried toward the shore, followed by the ever-present dog, Luke threw back his head and roared.

"Oh, Casey. You should see your face."

"Be careful, Luke Pierson. If you say one more word, I'll make you clean up this mess by yourself."

"Uh-uh. We had a bet, remember? And I won. So, excuse me while I take a nap. I'm sure you don't mind, since you have a lot to do here."

Stretching out on the blanket, he rolled to his side and closed his eyes.

While Casey packed away the scraps of food and dishes from their picnic, she was achingly aware of the man who slept so peacefully beside her. Finishing her chore, she sat down with her back to the rough bark of a tree, and watched Luke. She was glad she came with him today. He could make her laugh, and he could make her heart stop with a single look. Yet, she detected a wariness in him. Something, or someone, had hurt him. And the pain was still there at times in his eyes. And in Danny's.

She glanced toward the shore, where the little boy and the dog were bent over, examining something. She would give anything to erase the pain in those innocent eyes. He deserved love and happiness, and faith that everything would be all right.

Sighing, she stretched her arms above her head, then started to stand. Luke's hand snaked out, catching her ankle and pulling her down beside him.

"Oh." She gasped as she landed in a tangle of arms and legs. "You scared the daylights out of me," she muttered, pushing roughly against his chest.

"I just wanted to test your reflexes." His arms came around her, drawing her closer.

Casey was aware of the warmth of his body, of the strength in the arms and thighs pressed tightly to her. His breath feathered the hair at her temple as he brought his mouth to the pulse that beat there. Instinctively, she clung to him and kissed his throat.

"Oh, Miss Leary. I do approve of your reflexes," he murmured into a tangle of hair.

At her throaty laughter, Danny and Trouble joined the pile of bodies on the blanket. "Oh, boy. A wrestling match," Danny shouted, jumping on his father.

Trouble, eager to join in, leaped on Casey. With

howls of laughter, they rolled about the blanket until, exhausted, they moved apart. Trouble sat, his tail thumping, licking Casey's face. Luke watched with a smile as Casey stood and brushed grass and dog hairs from her slacks.

"I'm beginning to think that all of you play too rough for me," she said.

Luke caught her hand and pulled her down gently beside them. "Is this the little tomboy talking? The one who could beat five brothers?"

She grinned at Danny. "No, this is the one who lost a bet and had to clean up after your mess. And this is the thanks I get."

Luke turned to his son. "How can we thank Casey for cleaning up?"

Danny thought hard for a moment. "We could buy her an ice-cream sundae on the way home."

Casey laughed. "I like the way you think." Turning to Luke, she asked, "How about it? Are you going to feed my sweet tooth?"

"Yeah, Dad. Hot fudge, with lots of whipped cream."

"And nuts and chocolate sprinkles," Casey added while Danny nodded agreement.

"All right. Two against one. You win. Let's go. We'll find an ice-cream parlor on the way home."

Luke retrieved Danny's clothes, which had dried in the sun. While Casey carried the blanket, Luke took charge of the wicker basket. With the car loaded, they settled in for the long ride back to the city.

When they had only traveled about halfway, Luke

turned into a wide suburban avenue and parked the car.

Casey glanced up in surprise. "Why are we stopping here?"

"Because, Miss Leary, I promised you a hot-fudge sundae." He pointed to a line of shops. At the corner stood an old-fashioned ice-cream parlor.

Reluctantly leaving Trouble in the car, Danny danced ahead of them toward the shop. Inside, he stood with his nose pressed to the glass, studying the dozens of flavors of ice cream.

"I can't decide, Dad. I think I want whatever Casey's getting."

Luke laughed. "Me too. The decision is yours, Casey. We're in your hands."

Minutes later, they dug into hot-fudge sundaes topped with whipped cream, nuts, chocolate sprinkles, and a cherry. Luke sat back, a wide grin on his face, watching Casey eat. At last she set down her spoon and glanced up.

"Sweet tooth satisfied?" Luke asked.

She nodded. "That was wonderful. I'm definitely satisfied."

"Me too," Danny said, giving up in defeat. He wore a chocolate mustache.

Casey glanced at the ice cream left in his dish. "That was nice of you to save some for Trouble."

"Can I take the rest to him?"

She nodded. "We can't leave him out of this treat. He'd be so disappointed."

At the car, they waited while Trouble licked the last

of the ice cream from the disposable container. Then they piled into the car for the rest of the trip home.

Dusk was settling over the city when they reached it. Streetlights winked on. Danny climbed over the front seat and settled down on Casey's lap.

"Trouble's sleeping. He takes up the whole seat. Can I stay up here?"

"Of course." Casey's arms wrapped around the tired little boy, drawing him firmly against her. "I have an empty lap just waiting for you."

Burrowing his face into her neck, Danny snuggled against her and drowsed. Luke's gaze trailed the woman and his sleeping child.

"You look so natural with him, Casey."

She felt a tightness in her throat and, abruptly changing the subject, turned to stare out the window. "I love this time of the day. No longer light, not quite darkness. It's so still, so expectant, waiting for the night."

"Why haven't you married, Casey?"

There it was. The question she knew he would ask. The silence hung between them for so long that he turned to watch her.

Casey took a deep breath. Her voice was hushed out of consideration for the sleeping child. "There was a man. I've known him since we were children. We dated all through high school. I waited for him while he went off to college. David Clifton, Junior. I had chances to date other boys, but I wanted to be loyal."

"And while you were waiting faithfully, he was seeing someone else."

She shook her head. "Oh, no. David wasn't like that. He wouldn't—cheat on me."

"So what happened? You just decided you didn't love him?"

She turned to Luke. "No. Actually, he was the one who broke the engagement. We—each wanted something from marriage that the other was incapable of giving."

Luke's voice hardened. "He must be blind. You're the most giving woman I've ever met."

"You don't understand," she said patiently. "There are some things we can't give, even if we want to."

His head swiveled sharply. "Why are you defending him? Do you still love him?"

She was silent for so long that Luke felt his throat go dry. When at last she spoke, he felt a trembling sigh of relief.

"No. I don't still love him. I realize how lucky we were to discover our—differences before we married. So many people don't discover how badly mismatched they are until it's too late."

Luke gripped the wheel tightly. Yes, he thought. Some of us aren't so lucky. The thought of Lyn still brought the dull throb of pain to his temples. He turned the car to the sloping driveway of her house and slowed to a stop.

"I hate to disturb Danny," she murmured in the gathering darkness.

"He won't even wake up. Here." Luke took the sleeping child and lay him on the seat between them. Then he reached across the back of the seat and stroked her shoulder, smoothing away the tension in the taut cord of her neck. "This boyfriend . . ."

"David."

He paused, hating even to say the name. "David. Has he married?"

"Yes."

Luke took a cigarette from a pack and held a lighter to the tip. His hand shook from the anger he felt for this faceless man who had somehow hurt her. "You say you no longer love him. Then why are you still afraid to love again?"

She turned her face away. Her voice was muffled. "Because the problem was mine. And I still have it. I'll always have it."

"Problem? What problem?"

Casey stared at the glowing cigarette in the darkened car. She studied the angry profile of the man who had dared to ask her such personal questions. Taking a deep breath, she flung the words, hoping to say them quickly enough so that they would no longer hurt.

"David Clifton, Junior, wanted a little David Clifton the Third. He wanted a son and heir. And we discovered that I have this—inadequacy. You see Luke, I can't have children."

Deliberately, she opened the car door and held it until Trouble lumbered from the back seat. Then she closed it softly behind her. With her head held high, she mounted the steps of the front porch and opened the door.

Luke sat in stunned silence. Once, he had accused her of being too dedicated a career woman to want to bother with a husband and children. How his words must have wounded her.

He hurled the cigarette into the darkness and ran after her. At the doorway he caught her by the shoulders and dragged her roughly against him. With his lips pressed against her ear he rasped, "David Clifton, Junior is the biggest damn fool I've ever heard of. He's the loser, Casey, not you. You have a greater capacity to love than anyone I've ever met."

"Stop it, Luke. I'm well aware of my inadequacy."

His eyes narrowed. His voice was laced with steel. "Don't you ever say that word again." His fingers dug into the soft flesh of her upper arms. He shook her so hard that little strands of hair fell across one eye.

She gasped, but he seemed unaware of it. She could feel rage boiling through him, fighting for expression. He swore furiously and hauled her on tiptoe against his chest.

"You're worth a hundred David Cliftons. A thousand. You were too good for him. Sometimes I think you're too good to be true."

"Luke, please . . ."

"No. You listen to me, Casey. No one has the right to destroy another's self-esteem. He's the reason you've been hiding away from the world."

"I'm not hiding."

His grip tightened. "You've been holed up here with old people and children and animals who won't make any demands on your emotions. You've been avoiding any kind of man-woman relationship, because you're afraid of being hurt again. And you tell me you're not hiding?"

"Please, Luke. Let me go."

"No." White-hot anger blazed in his eyes. "You're a woman, Casey. A warm, loving, giving woman. And no one has the right to make you feel less."

She bit off her words with venom. "And I suppose you're just the man to show me how much of a woman I really can be?"

"Yes. If you'll let me."

His fingers bit into her flesh. At her little gasp, he suddenly relaxed his grip, then began massaging her shoulders tenderly.

She backed away as if the touch of him repelled her. "I expected a better line than that from you, Luke. Couldn't you come up with something original?" With a look of contempt, she hurried through the doorway. For emphasis, he heard the key turn in the lock.

He strode down the steps and leaned his forehead against the top of the car. For long moments he stood rigidly, before climbing inside. Then he sat, watching, as the lights went on upstairs. He lit another cigarette and thought about the woman inside the house. He hadn't meant to hurt her. She'd been hurt enough for one lifetime. He swore in frustration. The youngest of six children. A woman who adored children. A person who was capable of reaching out to so many different creatures with absolute, unselfish love. And she felt inadequate. Impotent fury boiled over again, and he pounded the steering wheel before starting the car.

His son sighed and rolled over. Luke listened to the regular sound of his breathing and found himself cursing life's ironies.

Chapter Seven

Casey pasted a bright smile on her face as she went about her morning routine. It had been a week since the picnic with Luke and Danny. Each day, when they arrived at the day-care center, she had managed to find something to occupy her time in another part of the house. Each evening, when Luke stopped by to pick up his son, she stayed at her desk, poring over the bills.

Hearing the arrival of the first children, she hurried to her office. This was the perfect time to catch up on her paperwork. She was not, she told herself earnestly, dodging Luke. She was simply a very busy person.

When the door to her office was thrown open without the courtesy of a knock, she looked up sharply. A scowling Luke stood in the doorway, his arms crossed over his chest, his feet planted firmly apart, as if poised for a fight.

"You've been avoiding me." He slammed the door behind him.

"Don't be ridiculous."

"Then why are you hiding back here?"

"Hiding! In case you haven't noticed, I have work to do. Now, if you'll excuse me."

He crossed the room and leaned his palms flat on her desk, obliterating the columns of figures in the ledger. With his face just inches from hers, he snarled, "You're hiding again, Casey. Holed up back here, away from reality."

She pushed back her chair and stood, hoping to escape his cutting anger. "I'm trying to run a business here, Luke. And I never seem to get caught up. I can do without your intrusion. Now please leave my office."

She swung away. Before she could take three steps, he was around her desk. Catching her roughly by the arm, he spun her to face him. "Tell me again you're not avoiding me."

She kept her gaze fixed on his tie, unable to meet his stern gaze. She spat out each word with venom. "I'm very busy. I am not avoiding you."

He lifted her chin, forcing her to stare into those smoky eyes. "Then have dinner with me tonight."

"No." She licked her lips and looked away. "I have a lot of paperwork to catch up on."

His voice lowered. "Tomorrow night, then."

She shook her head.

His hands dropped to his sides. She watched him cross the room. At the door, he stopped and turned.

"You might like to know that Danny's been opening

You know the thrill of escaping to a world of **EXOTIC LOCATIONS... EXCITING ADVENTURE... and ENDURING LOVE...**

Escape again...with 4 FREE novels and

**get more great Silhouette Romance novels
—for a 15-day FREE examination—
delivered to your door every month!**

Travel the globe in search of romance—and find it in the pages of Silhouette Romance novels. You can escape month after month with such all-time favorite authors as Brooke Hastings, Fern Michaels, Elizabeth Hunter, and Anne Hampson as your "guides."

Meet lively young heroines and share in their trials and triumphs...fascinating men you'll find as irresistible as the heroines do... and colorful supporting characters you'll feel you've known forever. They're all in Silhouette Romances—and now you can share every one of the wonderful reading adventures they provide.

FREE BOOKS

Start today by taking advantage of our special offer—4 brand new Silhouette Romance novels (a $7.80 value) *absolutely FREE* along with a free Mystery Gift. Just fill out and mail the attached order card.

AT-HOME PREVIEWS, FREE DELIVERY

After you receive your 4 free books and Mystery Gift, every month you'll have the chance to preview 6 more Silhouette Romance novels *before they're available in stores.* When you decide to keep them, you'll pay just $11.70, *with never an additional charge of any kind and with no risk!*

Cancel your subscription at any time simply by dropping us a note. In any case, the first 4 books and Mystery Gift are yours to keep.

EXTRA BONUS

When you take advantage of this offer, we'll also send you the Silhouette Books Newsletter FREE with each shipment. Every informative issue features news about upcoming titles, interviews with your favorite authors, and even their favorite recipes.

Get a Free
Mystery Gift, too!

**EVERY BOOK YOU RECEIVE WILL BE
A BRAND-NEW FULL-LENGTH NOVEL!**

CLIP AND MAIL THIS POSTPAID CARD TODAY!

NO POSTAGE
NECESSARY
IF MAILED
IN THE
UNITED STATES

BUSINESS REPLY CARD
FIRST CLASS PERMIT NO. 194 CLIFTON, N.J.

Postage will be paid by addressee

Silhouette Books
120 Brighton Road
P.O. Box 5084
Clifton, NJ 07015-9956

Escape with 4 Silhouette Romance novels (a $7.80 Value) and get a Mystery Gift, too!

Silhouette Romance ®

Silhouette Books, 120 Brighton Rd., P.O. Box 5084, Clifton, NJ 07015-9956

Yes, please send me FREE and without obligation, 4 brand new Silhouette Romance novels along with my Mystery Gift. Unless you hear from me after I receive my 4 FREE books, please send me 6 new Silhouette Romance novels for a free 15-day examination each month as soon as they are published. I understand that you will bill me a total of just $11.70, with no additional charges of any kind. There is no minimum number of books that I must buy, and I can cancel at any time. The first 4 books and Mystery Gift are mine to keep, even if I never take a single additional book.

NAME	
	(please print)
ADDRESS	
CITY	STATE ZIP

SIGNATURE (If under 18, parent or guardian must sign).

up to me. I think our day in the country was the key. Since then, he's been talking a lot about you and Patience and Trouble. He loves it here. This has become his home. You've made him feel safe and comfortable. Those were two ingredients that had been missing in his life for a while."

"I'm glad." Casey turned her back on him to stare out the window. "But as you once reminded me, Luke, he's your responsibility. I won't be conned into going out with you again out of some misguided sense of duty."

She heard the coldness in his tone. "I just thought you would care. Good-bye, Casey."

She didn't bother to turn around at the sound of the door closing. When she heard it open again, she turned, ready for another fight. Patience's black eyes glittered with amusement.

"Luke Pierson just went out of here looking like a wolf who smelled blood."

"An apt description." Casey walked back to her desk and sat down wearily.

"You don't look much better. What's between you two?" Patience sat down in one of the two chairs across from Casey's desk.

"Nothing."

"That's a lot of tension for nothing."

"He asked me out to dinner. I refused."

The black eyes flashed. "Seems to me you two have gone beyond the 'going out to dinner' stage."

Casey looked up sharply. "And what's that supposed to mean?"

Patience arched an eyebrow and gave her a knowing

smile. "I'm not blind. I can see how you look when he's around. And that man's been looking at you like a lovesick puppy ever since he first met you. You should see his face when he's watching you. Especially when he thinks no one is looking. If that isn't love, I don't know what is."

"Love." Casey gave a sound of disgust.

Patience watched her face carefully. Casey's lower lip trembled.

"Oh, Patience," she sighed, slamming shut her ledger and leaning her face in her hands. "What am I going to do?"

"About what?"

"About Luke. I made the mistake of telling him the truth last week. About my inability to have children."

"You did?" Incredulous, the old woman tapped the arm of the chair excitedly. She knew what a difficult thing that had to be for her young friend. Casey confided her problems to few people. Especially something as traumatic as the medical problem that left her incapable of conceiving. She always covered everything with a cheerful facade, giving the impression that her life was nearly perfect. But this was a big step. A step back to the world. "And?" she coaxed.

"And, as men will do," Casey said, using sarcasm to cover her pain, "he offered to make the supreme sacrifice and 'help me deal with my problem'. In his words, I'm a warm, caring woman who just needs a man in my life to make everything right again."

Gray eyebrows pulled together in a frown. "What makes you think he's lying?"

"Oh, Patience." The tears Casey had held back for a week brimmed to the surface and rolled down her cheeks. "It's such a tired line. Don't you see? Now that he knows the truth, it's all so easy for him. He can make love to me, without fear of any obligations. And when he's tired of me, he can walk away, knowing there will be no ties."

"Is that what you're worried about?"

The tears continued.

"You don't mean that, Casey." Patience came around the desk and hugged her fiercely. "After all these years, I think I'm a pretty good judge of people. I know Luke Pierson is an impatient, angry man. It looks to me like he's been through a lot. But I've seen his face when he looks at you, Casey. He couldn't hurt you. Here." She fumbled in her pocket and handed the young woman a lace handkerchief. "Blow."

While Casey blew her nose, Patience asked softly, "Do you love him?"

Casey nodded. Her voice was barely a whisper. "I've never met anyone who makes me feel the way Luke does. I think I love him, Patience." She stood and walked to the door. With her hand on the knob, she sighed. "But I loved David once, too. And where did it get me?"

She hurried away, eager for hard work, which would take her mind off her problems.

After she left, Patience walked to the window, staring at the lush spring colors in the yard. Love and springtime, she mused. Youth and loss of innocence. She'd led a full life. She'd taught school. Traveled to foreign lands. Made some lasting friendships. She thought she'd seen and heard it all. There were very few things she would do differently in her life. But if there were one truth she could give to Casey, it was this. Her life would have been very empty without love.

Casey kicked off her shoes and padded barefoot to the kitchen. She felt drained. She didn't even have the energy to fix anything to eat. Setting the kettle on the stove for tea, she walked to the bedroom to change. With her workday over, she peeled off her sweater and jeans and slipped into a white lace teddy. Over this she tied a white silk kimono that barely covered her, falling just below her hips.

The kettle whistled, and she hurried to the kitchen. While she was pouring the tea, the doorbell rang. Trouble began barking excitedly. She glanced at the clock. It was too late for appointments. The bell rang a second time, then a third.

With an impatient sigh, she scrambled barefoot down the stairs, with Trouble lumbering ahead.

Whoever it was now leaned on the bell, ringing it continually. Casey peered through the window, then angrily pulled open the door.

"Luke. You'll wake the entire neighborhood. What do you want?"

His gaze swept shapely legs, exposed beneath the kimono, then moved upward, liking the way the silk hugged her curves, exposing more than it covered. He held up a bulky bag. "I brought you some dinner."

"You never give up, do you?"

"Nope." He bent and ruffled Trouble's fur, then

nudged past her. "Yes, thanks, I believe I will come in."

She studied him for a moment, fighting the feelings that always overwhelmed her when she was close to him. Tonight, dressed in narrow jeans that rode low on his hips and a T-shirt that revealed his muscles, she was more aware of him than ever.

"I'm sorry, Luke. I've put in a long day. I'm really tired. I was just going to have some tea, and maybe read in bed."

"Okay. I'll join you." He grinned and walked toward the stairs.

With a sigh of exasperation, she hurriedly locked the door, then trailed up the stairs after him.

"I've seen you eat, Casey," Luke muttered, eyeing the cup of tea on the counter. "It takes a lot of fuel to keep you going. I'm afraid tea just isn't enough."

He opened the bag and began removing small cartons. Rummaging through the cupboards, he found some bowls and began spooning the contents of the cartons into them.

Casey crossed her arms over her chest and glowered at him. The wonderful, mouth-watering aroma of Chinese food began to fill the kitchen.

"I wasn't sure what you'd like, so I bought a little of everything." He glanced up in time to see her look of anticipation. "Of course, if you don't like Chinese food . . ."

"I love it." She walked closer, trying to hold onto her frown. "Is that moo goo gai pan?" She eyed tender chicken and Oriental vegetables.

He grinned. "Yes. And woo dip harr." He spooned

out butterfly shrimp sautéed with bacon and onions. He uncovered another carton. "A little almond boneless chicken. Plus some sweet-and-sour pork."

"Ooh." Casey dipped her fingers into the bowl, and Luke slapped it away with the spoon.

Eagerly, she began setting the table, completely forgetting her earlier anger.

Luke pulled a bottle of amber wine from the bag. "I promised to replace the wine we drank the last time, remember?"

"I told you you didn't have to." A smile lit her face. "But I'm glad you did." She retrieved two long-stemmed glasses, then sat down.

Luke poured the wine, tasted it, nodded in satisfaction, then filled her glass.

"Umm. Lovely," she murmured, her eyes suddenly alive. All her features had become more animated. Her earlier tiredness was completely erased.

Luke passed her a bowl of rice. Before long, their plates were heaped with wonderful Chinese delicacies.

Leaning back, Luke watched Casey over the rim of his glass. With her mouth filled, she glanced up. Their gazes locked. He smiled. She swallowed, then shook her head, laughing.

"How could I have thought I wasn't hungry? Oh, Luke, this is heavenly. " The smile touched his eyes, and she found herself thinking how wonderful he looked.

"Do you have room for dessert?" he asked when they had emptied most of the bowls.

She nodded and poured tea for both of them. Setting down a plate of almond tea cookies and little bowls of sherbet, he handed her a fortune cookie and took one for himself.

Breaking open the cookie, she read the little message, then laughed. "It says 'You are going on a long trip. It will be beneficial to the heart'." She grinned impishly. "I have no plans for open-heart surgery in the near future. And the farthest from home I've been lately is our drive in the country."

Luke broke open his cookie. He read the message, smiled, then handed it wordlessly to Casey.

She read it aloud. "'Man who has true love has all life's riches'." Glancing up, she said, "I'll settle for rubies."

Luke caught her hand across the table. Running his thumb over her fingers, he murmured almost to himself, "So long and delicate." He looked up. "You have an artist's hands, Casey. I think you're an incurable romantic. You can pretend to be cynical, but I know better." His voice lowered. "If I thought rubies would make you happy, I'd shower you with them."

Pulling her hand away, she stood and began to clear the table.

"Leave it," he said. "I want to walk with you in the moonlight." He stood and captured her hand again, and led her to the door.

At the sound of the door opening, Trouble and Duchess sprang to their feet and bounded outside, disappearing into the night shadows. A lavender mist hovered over the land. Casey felt the cool dampness of grass beneath her bare feet. Luke caught her hand, leading her toward the backyard. The scent of lilac and apple blossom lay heavy on the air.

"I noticed an old-fashioned glider under one of the apple trees, didn't I?"

Casey nodded. "Right over here. Gram used to love to sit out here, enjoying her yard. In the evenings, I'd settle her on the glider and read to her."

They sat down, and Luke dropped his arm around Casey's shoulders. The gentle motion was a soothing balm.

"How did your parents die?" Luke asked softly.

"An automobile accident. They were on their way to visit my brother. It was so shocking. That morning, we said good-bye. That evening, they were gone."

"Is that when you moved in here?"

She nodded. "I thought it would only be for a little while. But by the time I was ready for some independence, I realized how much Gram needed me."

"And I suppose by the time she died, there was David Clifton, Junior." Luke still found the name offensive. He had an unreasonable hatred for a man he'd never met.

"Yes. There was David. I think, more than anything else, I felt safe with him. Life with David would be . . ." She groped for the word. ". . . serene. No more Greek tragedies. No challenges. Just smooth sailing."

"Sounds dull."

She turned to him in the darkness, hearing the edge to his voice. "I suppose, for a man like you, who wanders about the country in search of an elusive dream, my whole life must seem pretty dull."

He brushed his knuckles across her cheek, feeling

the incredible softness of her skin. At his touch, something tightened deep inside her.

"Casey Leary, I find you vibrant, enticing, bewitching. Of all the challenges I've faced, you are by far the most exciting and the most difficult."

He leaned toward her, his face shadowy and mysterious in the moonlight. Instantly, she was aware of the warmth of his body. The faint scent of lime soap and after-shave became even more exotic than the spring flowers whose fragrance wafted around them. His fingertips were rough against her skin, drawing her closer. She waited, heart stilled, breathless, for the first touch of his lips on hers.

The kiss was as delicate as a flower petal drifting on a gentle breeze. His breath mingled with hers. As her lips parted, he deepened the kiss, bringing his arms around her, drawing her firmly into his embrace.

Luke had promised himself before he came here this evening that he would be silly and teasing and friendly. Nothing more. Casey's emotions weren't up to dealing with passion. And his own emotions in the past year had been too badly battered to deal with the intricacies of passion. What they both needed right now was gentle, casual friendship. Nothing more.

But her kiss—hesitant, trembling—hinted of a simmering passion just below the calm surface. And the knowledge that he could take her over the edge of that cool control was tantalizing. What he failed to consider was his own burning need, a need too long denied.

One more kiss, he thought as his lips moved over hers. One more, before he walked away.

Small, firm breasts were crushed against his chest. Her lush hair lifted on the night breeze, kissing his cheek, inviting his touch.

"Oh God, Casey," he moaned against her mouth.

She sought to comfort him. Lifting her hand to his face, she traced the outline of his firm jaw, then ran a fingertip lightly over his lips.

Her gentle touch was his undoing. He could feel his heart leap, his blood boil. With an almost brutal fury, he pulled her head back and covered her lips with his.

For a moment, fear paralyzed her. An alarm sounded in her mind. But in the next moment, her fear was replaced with a wild, almost primitive passion. She couldn't think. She could only feel the flame that raged through him, arousing her until she was on fire.

Luke felt a madness taking over his control. He had to touch her. He had to know all the secrets of the woman in his arms.

The silk robe and the scant lace teddy were no barrier to his probing fingers. His hand found her breast, small and firm. Her heart was pounding, matching the erratic rhythm of his own. Her excitement fueled his fever.

No one had ever made her feel like this. No man had ever touched her as Luke did. As his rough hand pulled away the silk kimono, his lips trailed her neck, her shoulder, then covered her mouth once more as his fingers caressed her breast.

She moaned softly and clung to him, spurred on by

his need. Her mouth was avid and her kiss became more demanding.

There was no trace of tenderness in him now. His body was tense, hard. The fingertips that touched her were rough. His teeth nipped, his lips sought. And all the while, she matched his strength, his need, his fury.

Then, suddenly, Luke caught her by the shoulders. One moment, he had been caught up in the kiss. The next, abruptly, he was holding her away.

She blinked, then stared questioningly up at him. In her eyes he saw surprise, then confusion. Her lips were moist and swollen from his kiss. Her one shoulder was bare, the pale skin so seductively translucent in the moonlight that he had to fight the overwhelming desire to touch his lips to it.

With a great effort of will, he straightened the silk kimono, smoothing it over her shoulder.

"Luke, I . . ."

"Shh." He touched her lips with a fingertip, silencing her. "I'm sorry, Casey. It's time for me to leave. Past time."

He stood. She continued to sit on the glider, staring up at him.

At the far side of the yard, Trouble bayed at the moon. A ghostly figure leaped to the back of the glider, then curled itself into a ball.

She watched until Luke merged with the shadow of the house. With a long, drawn-out sigh that seemed to tremble from her lips, she reached a hand over to smooth the cat's fur.

"Oh, Duchess," she whispered. "How can I keep fighting these feelings?"

The cat purred beneath her hand. Clouds scudded across the sky, completely covering the moon. Casey leaned her head back while the glider gently swayed. There was an aching emptiness within her that nothing would satisfy.

Chapter Eight

"Casey." Patience's voice broke her concentration. "There's a man out here from the city. He said you were expecting him."

"Thanks, Patience. Send him in."

Hurriedly, Casey slipped her ledgers and bills into a desk drawer and stood to greet the inspector.

On this gray, spring day he wore a trench coat over dark slacks and a white shirt. Poking from his coat pocket was a small, folded umbrella. Prepared for any emergency, thought Casey wearily. In his hand he carried a clipboard. Sparse gray hair was combed over an obvious bald spot. His face looked rumpled, lived in. Faded blue eyes regarded her with unconcealed curiosity.

"I believe you complained about your tax assess-

ment, Ms. Leary. The city sent me over to reassess
your property. I've gone over it very carefully."

"Thank you." Casey smiled, hoping to make a good
impression. "As you can see by last year's bill, my tax
assessment this year has doubled."

He ignored the chair she offered and stood beside
her desk, allowing his gaze to wander about the small
room and its comfortable furnishings.

"Last year, this was a private residence. This year,
it's a small business."

"But double the taxes?" Casey steadied herself
against the desk, feeling the first twinges of unease
caused by his imperious tone.

"It is now a revenue-producing property, Ms. Leary.
You are deriving an income from this place. Therefore,
the tax structure has changed." He cleared his throat.
"Now that I've had a chance to thoroughly inspect the
premises, I feel that if anything, we've given you a
break. We could actually charge you much more."

She clutched her hands at her sides. Her voice
sounded oddly strangled. "Then I guess you won't be
persuaded to reduce the tax bill."

"Hardly." He shook his head for emphasis. "You're
getting a very fair break from the city." Extending his
hand, he added, "I'll make my report this afternoon.
Since there are no recommended revisions on the bill,
we'll expect you to pay the amount shown on your
copy. Good day, Ms. Leary."

Casey waited until the door closed behind him before
slumping into her chair. For long minutes she sat,
staring out at the overcast sky, studying the rolling
lawn, seeing the blossoming fruit trees, the masses of

blooming lilacs. Then her eyes misted over, and she wiped at them angrily before forcing herself into action.

Running a finger through her personal phone directory, she stopped at a familiar name. Without pausing, she dialed the number, listened to the ringing at the other end of the line, then took a deep breath.

"Mr. Melton. Casey Leary. About that Florence Epson painting you wanted for your collection. Would you like to come over this afternoon and look at it? I'd be interested in hearing your price."

Replacing the phone, she buried her face in her hands and allowed herself a few private moments of grief.

"Casey. Come with me. I'd like you to see something." Patience's voice, normally calm and low-pitched, fairly trembled with excitement.

Following the older woman along the hallway, Casey paused in the doorway of the parlor, which had been converted into a large playroom.

Wooden blocks lay scattered in heaps about the room. Danny and a four-year-old, Jamie, were deep in concentration, building what appeared to be a fort.

"That's nice," Casey muttered, wondering why such a typical activity should cause her assistant such excitement.

"Stay and visit a while," Patience urged. The tone of her voice said more than her words.

Intrigued, Casey knelt down and began chatting with the two little boys.

"Hi, Jamie. What are you building?"

The boy looked up, picked up several more blocks,

then turned his attention to the unfinished job. "Danny and I are building a city. I'm making a fire hall. When I grow up, I want to ride on a fire truck, and climb ladders up burning buildings."

"A fireman. That's nice. Will you mind getting up in the middle of the night when there's a fire?"

"Not if I can zoom around on a fire truck."

Casey turned. "What are you building, Danny?"

The little boy picked up a block which had tumbled from the top and carefully replaced it before looking up. "I'm building a house."

"Like the one you live in?"

"No. We live in a 'partment. This is a real house, with a yard full of trees and flowers."

"Who's living in it?" Casey watched as he formed an outer perimeter with blocks.

"Me and my dad. And lots of cats and dogs, and grandmas and grandpas. And Jamie," he added as an afterthought.

"Is Jamie going to be like your brother?"

Danny grinned at the other little boy. "No. Jamie's my friend." Handing Jamie one of his own blocks, he said, "Here. You need this for your door. And I've already finished my chimney."

Patience shot Casey a meaningful look. Casey nodded, pleased that Danny was willing to share.

Danny turned to Casey. "Want to come in my house?"

"Yes, I'd like that. Can you tell me what the rooms are?"

Taking her hand, he stepped carefully over the first pile of blocks. "This is the front door."

Casey followed him, gingerly avoiding tripping over the blocks.

"And this is the kitchen. My dad's cooking dinner. He's a good cook. Tonight we're having hot dogs."

"Of course. Your favorite. Nothing but the best. Gourmet fare."

Danny nodded without understanding the fancy words. "And in here is my bedroom. From my window I can see all the stars in the sky."

"You mean you have a glass roof?" she asked teasingly.

"No. But it's way up at the top of the house, almost in the sky. What's at the top of your house, Casey?"

"An attic. That's a big bare room where I store some old furniture, and albums and things I can't use anymore but can't bear to part with. Would you like to see it some time?"

He nodded solemnly. "Oh, boy! Yes. And that's where I'm going to sleep. At the very top of the house, in the attic, so I can see the stars."

"Oh. That's very smart."

He beamed at her compliment.

"What's this room?" She stepped over the wall of blocks.

"That's my dad's bedroom. And this is our bathroom. I like to watch my dad shave."

"Is this the living room?" Casey asked, pointing to the last room.

"That's for you and Trouble and Duchess," Danny said matter-of-factly.

"We're going to live there too?"

"You already do, silly. This is your house."

Caught off guard, Casey could only stare a moment. Recovering her composure, she smiled at him. "So you like this house better than your apartment? Why?"

"'Cause it always smells good, like cookies, and clean stuff. And it's got grandmas. And Trouble. And friends like Jamie." He smiled shyly. "And best of all, you."

Casey's heart lodged somewhere in her throat. Kneeling down, she hugged the little boy before walking quickly from the room.

Shortly after, Patience knocked on Casey's office door. Taking a chair, she asked, "Have you had time to analyze all that?"

"Some of it was a little too close to me, I'm afraid. It's hard to be objective. But I certainly caught the smile in Danny's eyes."

"What about the fact that Danny was able to share with Jamie?" Patience asked.

"Yes. That was significant. He's beginning to trust enough to form friendships with the others. And to share. Not only the blocks, but the people. He's willing to share all his grandmas with the others. That's a big step for Danny."

"And the house?"

"That really threw me," Casey admitted. "I think it means that he's beginning to accept his time here, apart from his father's work day, as normal."

"We both know it's much more than that," Patience said, watching Casey's face. "This house is a symbol of love and security. All of us here are beginning to represent home and family to Danny. And you're a big part of all this."

"I can't wait to tell his father how much progress Danny's made," Casey said suddenly. "I'm sure it'll be a relief to know how well his son has adjusted to his life in Chicago."

Patience nodded and stood. "By the way, there's a Mr. Melton here. Says you're expecting him."

Casey's smile vanished. "Thanks, Patience. Send him in."

As she left the room, Patience stared dubiously at the tall, distinguished man who nodded formally before closing the door.

"Miss Leary. I'm so glad you've had a change of heart. May I see it again before we talk business?"

That was all Patience overheard before walking away. Strange, she could usually pinpoint most of the officials who called on Casey. City inspectors had a certain disdainful look. And the salesmen who pitched their wares, from toys to cleaning supplies, often wore a bright, artificial smile. But this man, this stranger, fitted none of the categories she could think of. He had obviously come here on business. She shrugged and walked away. That was Casey's realm.

Casey led the way up the stairs to her private rooms. Dressed in a pair of frayed cutoffs and a T-shirt, she seemed an odd contrast to the man in the impeccably tailored suit and conservative silk tie.

In the doorway, she paused and allowed him to precede her into the large sitting room. His gaze swept fleetingly over the Persian rug, the wall of bookshelves, and the elegant black lacquer Chinese cabinet, then locked on the painting.

Wordlessly, he stood, his fingers laced at his waist, carefully studying the painting he had so long coveted. Bold splashes of intense color seemed to glow on the canvas. The painting intensified the colors in the room —the multihued rug, the flowers in a crystal vase. Because of the painting's lush beauty, the entire room seemed alive with color.

When he turned to her, his look was radiant. "It is as clear, as concise, as brilliant as I had remembered. It will stand out in my collection." There was a subdued eagerness in his manner. "Shall we go to your office now, Miss Leary, and discuss terms?"

She nodded, carefully averting her gaze from the framed painting that had been her gift of love on her grandmother's ninety-first birthday.

In her office, the elegantly attired gentleman named a figure. Casey swallowed, then nodded her assent. Quickly, before she had a chance to change her mind, he reached into his breast pocket and produced a check.

Accepting it, she said softly, "If you like, Mr. Melton, you may take the painting with you now. That way, you won't have to wait another day to enjoy it." And she wouldn't have to stare at it tonight, feeling the burden of guilt over what she had done.

"That's very kind of you, Miss Leary. I have the very spot for it." His smile grew. "Anticipating your generosity, I have my assistants waiting in a van outside."

Casey slipped the check into her drawer and sat stiffly, hearing the muffled sounds of footsteps on the stairs. When Mr. Melton returned, with two workmen trailing, the painting now carefully wrapped for the journey to his home, Casey forced herself to show no emotion.

"Good-bye, Miss Leary. And thank you again. You've made me a very happy man."

She accepted his firm handshake and forced a too-bright smile. "I know how much you'll enjoy it, Mr. Melton. Good-bye."

Patience watched Casey accompany the distinguished-looking man to the front door. Behind them, she saw the workmen carrying a wrapped painting, handling it with great care.

A moment later, she saw Casey hurry to her office. Her face showed the strain of the transaction. The office door closed with resounding force.

By midafternoon, the sky was as dark as night. The rain, which had threatened all day, now began in earnest. The gloom of the storm affected everyone. Casey moved through the rooms, helping her assistants invent games that would keep the children busy and happy. For the four- and five-year-olds, there was a story time, with puppets to act out the story. The two- and three-year-olds were playing games with sturdy trucks and tricycles. Infants and toddlers were being soothed in rocking chairs, as gentle classical music played in the background.

"Do you really think he'll grow up loving Bach?" Patience smiled at Casey as she rocked the infant in her arms.

"How can he miss? All his life, he'll connect these

lovely strains to comfort, and gentle motion, and contentment.

"Always the psychologist." The old woman bent to nuzzle his temple.

"I'm going to the kitchen to whip up some special treats," Casey announced. "If this turns into a full-blown storm, some of the parents may be late."

Soon she produced bowls of sliced fresh fruit—orange segments, peach and banana slices, and diced apple. For the younger ones, there were dishes of fruit gelatin. And for the infants, fresh fruit juice. The wonderful aroma of cookies baking in the oven wafted through the rooms, sending several of the older children racing to the kitchen to peer over Casey's shoulder the minute she opened the oven door. When the storm finally hit, with earthshaking thunder and jagged slashes of lightning, the children were too busy enjoying their treats to be alarmed.

Trouble, huddling beneath the table, had to be coaxed out by Danny. Feeling the tremors that signified the dog's terror, Danny looked up at Casey with alarm.

"What's he scared of, Casey?"

"He's afraid of the sound of thunder, I think. His reaction is always the same. Maybe he got locked out in a storm when he was just a little pup."

She smiled gently at the sight of the tiny boy who sought to console the huge dog. With his arms around Trouble's neck, Danny buried his face in soft fur and murmured words of endearment.

The lights flickered several times, causing shrieks among the youngsters. The elderly assistants glanced uneasily from time to time, but showed no outward emotion at the fury of the storm.

Casey stood at the French doors which opened to the backyard. The fruit trees swayed and dipped, their branches lashing out under the ferocity of the wind and rain. Tall iris and peony lay flattened, many twisted and broken. How could the delicate blossoms survive such a battering? Wind tore at the glider where she and Luke had kissed, setting it in motion. Rain lashed the windows and roared through downspouts, causing raging little rivers along the sides of the old house.

Casey pulled the drapes shut to blot out the storm's fury and switched on more lights.

The storm lasted nearly an hour before moving on. In its path, the heavy winds wreaked destruction, leaving broken tree limbs and power lines that had been snapped like thread. When at last it blew over, it left leaden skies and a steady downpour.

Soon moving headlights along the curving driveway signaled the arrival of the first of the parents. Casey and her assistants prepared for the rush of departure.

Figures darted through the puddles left by the storm. Some carried umbrellas. Some held newspapers over their heads as they hurried to the porch. Added to their shouts and calls were the squeals of children as they clasped hands and dashed back to their waiting cars.

When there were only three children left, Casey turned to Patience. "I can't wait any longer for Luke Pierson to arrive. There's too much I need to do in my office. When he gets here, Patience, would you send him back there?"

The older woman looked up from the shoelace she was tying for a toddler and nodded.

There was one brief knock before her office door was flung open. Casey looked up with a smile. The smile faded at the sight of Luke.

He had removed his suit jacket and tie. His soaked shirt clung to him, revealing the outline of dark hair on his chest. The sleeves were rolled above his elbows. The driving rain had plastered his black hair to his head. Little droplets trickled down his cheeks, almost like tears. His eyes were dark and stormy. His stance was so tense that Casey was reminded of the first time she had seen him.

In agitation, he ran a hand through his wet hair. "Patience said you wanted to talk to me."

"Yes. I thought you might like a progress report on Danny."

"Not tonight, Casey. It will have to wait." The words were clipped.

"But it's such good news, Luke." Her voice softened. "From the look of you, I'd say you could use some good news tonight."

"Today has been so bad, I can't think of anything you could say to make it better." His tone had the sting of bitterness. "If you don't mind, I'd like to take Danny home now."

"But Luke, there were some significant changes in Danny's behavior today. I think you should know how far he's come." Casey stood and walked around her desk. Moved by Luke's utter weariness, she reached out to gently touch his arm.

"Save it, Casey." He took a step back, avoiding her touch. "Tell me about it another time."

"I don't understand." With her hands on her hips, she faced him. "Don't you even care?"

For a moment, there was no sound in the room. Outside, the rain pelted the window. A violent oath escaped Luke's lips, and she stared at him in stunned surprise. Suddenly gripping her arms, he dragged her closer until her face was just inches from his. "Sometimes I used to think I was the only one who cared about that boy. When we were hurt, abandoned, without a soul to care about us, we had each other. We've always had each other. And there are times even now I don't think we need anyone else. Especially a meddlesome, good samaritan who's going to deluge us all with warm smiles."

"Luke." At his cruel words, she froze.

Releasing his grip, he clutched his hands fiercely at his sides and stared at her shocked expression. Wordlessly, he turned away. When he finally spoke, his words were muffled. "Forgive me, Casey. I didn't mean that. I'm just not fit for civilized people today."

He turned back and studied her grim features. With his voice little more than a whisper, he said, "I can't talk to you right now about Danny. Maybe by tomorrow I'll be better."

"What's happened, Luke?" Her eyes, masked by pain, appealed to him for some way to understand his strange behavior.

For long moments he was silent, staring down into her upturned face. With a deep sigh of resignation, he muttered, "Lyn called. She's here in Chicago. She wants to see Danny."

Bewilderment clouded Casey's features. "Lyn? I don't understand. Who is this Lyn, Luke?"

His voice turned to ice. "Sorry. I thought I'd mentioned her before. Lyn was my wife. Danny's mother."

Chapter Nine

In stunned silence, Casey watched Luke's retreating back as he stalked from her office. The door swung shut behind him, cutting off the voices, the children's laughter, the sounds of life that echoed through the old house.

Too many confusing thoughts and images crowded her mind as she walked to the window and studied the darkness, thoughts and images that swirled like the angry clouds overhead.

Had Luke ever said his wife was dead? she wondered. *There is no Mrs. Pierson.* She could recall those words, and the fury with which he had hurled them. And she, always eager to embrace the homeless, always willing to accept simple truths, had decided that Danny was a motherless child.

Lyn. A lovely name. Was she very beautiful? Casey frowned, deep in thought. Lyn, Luke's wife, Danny's mother, was here in Chicago. Did that mean that she had followed Luke and Danny? Luke said she wanted to see her son. Casey bit her lip. A natural enough request. Why, then, was Luke so upset?

Pacing the floor, Casey tried to think of a single instance when Luke or Danny had mentioned Lyn's name. There wasn't one that Casey could recall. They seemed to share a conspiracy of silence. It was as if she had been erased from their memories. No wonder she had thought the woman dead.

"Casey."

She whirled at the sound of Patience's muffled voice, followed by a knock on the office door.

"Yes." She hurried across the room.

"We're ready to roll whenever you are."

Astonished, Casey glanced at her watch. "Sorry. I had no idea it was so late. I meant to help pick up the toys."

"No problem. Everything's taken care of."

Casey caught up her purse and keys and followed her elderly friend to the van, where the others sat waiting.

Patience climbed in the front seat and turned slightly to study Casey's stiff profile while she drove. Casey maintained a tense silence. When the van was finally empty of its passengers except for the two of them, Patience broke through her reverie.

"How did Luke Pierson react to the news of Danny's progress?"

"I—" Casey paused. "I didn't get a chance to tell him."

"But I sent him back to your office."

Casey pulled the van to the curb and turned to meet the questioning gaze. "He was—running too late to discuss his son tonight."

Patience fumbled with her door key, then snapped her purse shut. "How about a cup of tea before you go home?"

Casey paused only a moment, then nodded and switched off the ignition. "I'd like that."

Inside the tidy apartment, while Patience hurried to the tiny kitchen to put on the kettle, Casey prowled, stopping to study the photographs and mementos that crowded walls and tabletops. Bending closer, she peered at a family portrait showing a younger, smiling Patience and her husband, and their son and daughter-in-law with their infant son.

Patience paused in the doorway. A loving smile lit her features. "Aren't they beautiful?"

Casey nodded. She knew that Patience was a widow. Indicating the others, she asked, "Where are they now?"

The older woman moved closer and picked up the framed picture, holding it to the light. "My husband died shortly after this was taken. I've always been so glad we had this portrait. Six years later, my son died. Too young," she said softly. "He was much too young." Turning bright eyes to Casey, she said, "My daughter-in-law, Janet, married again. They live in Arizona. He's a fine man, an engineer. She writes often."

"And your grandson?"

Very carefully, almost reverently, Patience replaced

the portrait. Straightening, she said softly, "He was a pilot in Vietnam. He flew thirty-two missions before he was shot down. Janet sent me one of the medals he was awarded posthumously." She pointed to a small framed military award beside a picture of a handsome young pilot.

"Oh, Patience," Casey sighed, touching her friend's arm. "I never knew. Your son. Your grandson. How could you bear it?"

The older woman gave her a gentle smile. "When you first met me, I was feeling very—bewildered. Alone. A strange city. A depressing sense of uselessness. My loss was too painful to talk about." The smile grew. "Then gradually, thanks to your friendship, I found my balance." She touched her young friend's shoulder. "We all have things we have to bear. And we all do it the same way. By taking them a day at a time. Time," she said, "is the great healer. Pain becomes dulled. The rough edges grow smooth."

Turning toward the kitchen, she said in a firm tone, "Come on. The kettle's whistling. Let's have that tea."

Along with the tea there were thick slabs of French bread, wedges of sharp cheese, and slices of smoked ham.

"Why didn't you talk to Luke Pierson about his son?" Patience asked.

"He was so distraught about something that happened today, he didn't want to talk about Danny."

The old woman's head came up sharply. "Did he say what was wrong?"

Casey nodded. "It seems his wife is here in Chicago, asking to see Danny."

"Wife! Didn't you say Danny had no mother?"

Casey's lips thinned. "That was my assumption. A wrong one, I see now. But Luke had said there was no Mrs. Pierson." She shrugged. "I just assumed she had died."

"Apparently Luke isn't happy about her arrival." Patience stared knowingly at Casey. "Or her request to see her son."

"That's what puzzles me," Casey said quietly. "Oh, Patience, how could he deny her the right to see her own child?" She stood abruptly, needing to be busy.

Seeing Casey's agitation, Patience filled the sink with hot, sudsy water and began to wash the dishes. Picking up a towel, Casey dried them vigorously.

"We don't know the facts of this, Casey. There are always reasons why people act the way they do."

"But he wasn't even civil. I could see the rage building in him. He seemed about to explode."

Patience drained the water and dried her hands. "Give him some time to get used to the idea of her being here, Casey. He'll calm down."

The slender shoulders shrugged off her words. "It doesn't matter to me what he does. It's his life. Luke Pierson is a big boy now. He can make all the mistakes he wants. And I won't care one way or the other."

Blackbird eyes sparkled with amusement. "Tell that to someone who doesn't know you as well as I do. You've gone beyond that now, Casey. Luke and Danny are important to you. Like it or not, you're deeply involved in their problems."

"You're wrong. I—care about them. The way I care about all the children and parents involved in the day-care center. But I have no intention of getting involved in their lives. You know I don't intend to get caught up in another relationship, Patience. It's taken me a long time to get over David. I'm not foolish enough to put myself through that again. I'm just not strong enough to endure that much emotional pain again."

Patience hung the dish towel. "Come on. Let's take our tea in the living room."

"No, thank you. I can't." Casey grimaced, suddenly annoyed at herself for burdening her dear friend with her troubles. "I'm leaving now. I need some quiet time to think."

Following her to the door, Patience touched her young friend's arm. "Stop hating David for wanting something you couldn't give. David wanted a son and heir, Casey. That was his right."

Seeing the pain that clouded Casey's features at the mention of past hurts, the older woman said softly, "Some people foolishly think that their children will somehow make them immortal. Maybe I thought that once. But we can't see the future." She swallowed, then plunged on. "It isn't important whether or not we leave behind offspring. What matters is how we've lived our lives. Whether we've made a contribution. Paid some dues. Whether we've loved unselfishly. That's the best thing we can leave the world." She touched Casey's arm. "Love. The more we give it, the more we get it back. Don't deny yourself the pleasure of love because you somehow feel you'll be cheating a man unless you can give him a child." She sighed. "Oh,

Casey. The right man will recognize all the love you have to give."

Casey was silent for long moments, then bent to brush her lips over the soft cheek. "Thanks. For the tea and sympathy. But most of all, for being my friend. Good night."

Patience stood in the doorway watching as the slender figure entered the van. Red taillights glowed in the darkness as the vehicle disappeared down the street.

The rain had ended. Behind the storm, a cool front had moved in, chilling the spring air. A brisk breeze had blown away the last of the dark clouds, leaving the night crystal clear. Stars twinkled in the midnight sky and a tiny sliver of moon seemed to hang suspended, just above the trees.

Casey, wrapped in a thick terry robe, clicked off the television and picked up a book. A short time later she tossed it aside and padded barefoot to the kitchen. Rummaging through the refrigerator, she searched for something to satisfy her restlessness. Nothing looked tempting enough to heat. She didn't have the energy to make something challenging.

The ringing of the doorbell below shattered the silence. Trouble, his sleep disturbed, lumbered ahead of her down the stairs.

At the door she peered through the window, then pulled the door open.

"Luke. It's past midnight."

He stood on the threshold, looking uncertain. His gaze swept her features for some sign of the hurt he had inflicted earlier. "I saw your lights and knew you were still awake. May I come in?"

Undecided, she paused, then reluctantly stepped aside. Trouble's tail wagged in delight at the company. Poking his head outside, he searched for the little boy who usually accompanied this man. Seeing no one else, he backed up, allowing Casey to close the door.

As they climbed the stairs, she asked, "Who's watching Danny?"

"My neighbor. She often comes over to stay with him after I put him to bed."

"What are you doing out at this time of night?"

"I couldn't sleep. I was out driving around. Just thinking." He cleared his throat. "No. That's not the whole truth." He touched her arm and felt her stiffen at his touch. Instantly, he dropped his hand to his side. "The fact is, I needed to talk to you. I was hoping you'd still be awake."

In the sitting room, she nodded toward the bar. "Would you like a drink?"

He walked over and opened a bottle. "Care to join me?"

"Yes. Whatever you're having."

Handing her the glass, Luke was careful not to touch her fingers. He noticed that she quickly moved away, as if she too had decided to avoid any physical contact.

They stood apart at the wide window, staring down at the rainwashed scene below. It was easier than looking at each other.

She sipped the drink, feeling the sharp bite of scotch on her tongue.

"Was there much damage from the storm?" Luke's gaze took in the broken tree limbs, the flattened, twisted flowers.

"Some. Vern and I should be able to clean up most of it by tomorrow. The hardiest trees and plants always manage to survive." And the hardiest people, she thought. The sound of her own words brought home Patience's meaning. A day at a time, we manage to survive each of life's storms.

"You must have had your hands full when the storm hit. Were the kids afraid?"

She shook her head. "We kept them pretty busy. I think they were more excited than frightened. They probably looked on it as a real adventure."

"Danny just mentioned in passing that the lights flickered. Other than that, I didn't hear a word about the storm. He was too busy talking about the special treats, the cookies you baked, the games he played."

Leaning a hip against the windowsill, he turned toward her. "You're all he talks about, Casey."

She avoided meeting his gaze. "I'm glad he likes it here. Would you like that progress report now?"

Luke nodded, watching her eyes while she spoke.

"Patience and I can see real changes in Danny. He's making friends. He's willing to share, not just toys, but more importantly, people. He's willing to share our time. That's a sign that he's beginning to trust, Luke. He's confident that we'll be here tomorrow and the next day. Don't you see?"

Luke was silent for long moments. Slowly he nodded.

Casey continued softly. "It's so important for Danny to trust adults again."

He tensed. "I want to explain about Lyn."

Casey set her glass down and, for the first time, deliberately met his look. She was angry. Her look was cool and penetrating. "You let me think she was dead."

Luke took a long pull on his drink, then said, "I never meant to give you the wrong impression. In the beginning, I was just too angry to speak about it. Then, when I realized what you thought, I didn't bother to explain because it was a personal affair. I thought it had nothing to do with you. Now I realize that in order to help Danny, you need to know all the facts. But, Casey, I never lied. Danny has no mother."

When she was about to say something, he held up a hand to interrupt her, then went on.

"A year ago, Lyn walked out on Danny and me."

Casey gasped, feeling a pain as sharp as any knife thrust. What she wouldn't give to have a son like Danny, a husband as loving as Luke.

Luke's voice was a monotone. "Lyn was offered a job doing some modeling. She said she wanted the chance to see if she could make it big in New York."

"Did she ask you and Danny to go along, or at least ask you to wait?"

He shook his head and stared down into the amber liquid in his glass. "She wanted to be free. A husband and baby would only be in the way."

Casey was silent for a long moment, seeing the familiar look of pain in Luke's eyes. "Has she found the success she went after?"

"I don't know. And frankly, I don't care." Casey heard the thread of steel in his voice. "Lyn doesn't exist for us any more. She got what she wanted. Her freedom."

"But she's Danny's mother. That fact will never change, Luke."

"She gave birth to him. Nothing more. That woman walked out of his life without ever looking back. In a whole year, this is the first word we've heard from her. And she has the gall to ask to visit with Danny."

"You're going to grant her request, aren't you, Luke?"

"No!"

Casey stared at him in horror. "She has that right."

"She has no rights." His icy tone sent a tremor along her spine. "She gave up all rights the day she walked out that door."

"Oh, Luke," Casey said softly. "I can understand how you feel. But all that bitterness inside you will eat away at you until you have no warmth, no tenderness left. You can't let that anger, that fury, destroy you. You have to find a way to forgive." At his strangled sound, she touched his arm. "Forgive Lyn. Then accept the fact that she can't love the way you do." Casey suddenly thought about herself and David. "You both wanted something from your marriage that the other couldn't give."

"I can forgive what she did to me. Frankly, she did me a favor. I might have spent the rest of my life with someone that . . ." He shook his head. "But I can't forgive what she did to Danny."

"Then don't make it worse." Casey assumed her most persuasive tone. "Luke, a child's strongest impressions about himself come from his parents. It's important for Danny's self-esteem that he be given the chance to visit with his mother. Although he never speaks about her, he has a natural curiosity about her. Let him satisfy that curiosity. All the work you've done, all the lessons you've taught him, won't be destroyed. She won't change him in a visit. Or in series of visits."

She watched his eyes, gray and opaque, narrowing in thought. "Even if Lyn finds success, she'll always carry a burden of guilt. But you have Danny's love, his respect. You can afford to be generous."

He stared down at her face, clean of all makeup, so fresh and beautiful to him. Mentally, he traced her full lower lip, and he clenched his hand to keep from reaching a fingertip to her mouth. Those beautiful amber eyes were guileless, imploring him to heed her words. She was so good, so loving, she almost made him believe in the impossible. She cleansed him. She made him feel better than he really was.

When his silence grew, Casey turned away and picked up her glass. "You haven't heard a word I've said, have you, Luke?"

As she crossed the room, he watched her until his gaze was suddenly caught by something. He stared at the wall behind her.

"What happened to the painting?"

She stared guiltily at the faded square on the wall.

In swift strides he crossed the room and caught her by the shoulders.

"Where's the Epson painting, Casey?" His words were taut, angry.

Her eyes looked huge in her delicate face. Her skin seemed even paler. "It's gone."

"I can see that it's gone. Where?" Without realizing it, he shook her.

"I—" She licked her lips. "I sold it. To a collector."

"Why?" He stared down at her and with one hand caught her chin, forcing her to meet his angry look.

"It's none of your business, Luke." She tried to break free of his grasp, but he tightened his hold.

"Why, Casey? I'm not letting go until you tell me."

"I have bills overdue. The taxes on this house doubled this year. I've been dipping into Gram's trust. Soon there'll be nothing left. And then I'll have to give up on my dream." She struggled free and said with a catch in her voice, "It was only a painting."

"A painting you loved."

Her words were muffled against her hands. "Not as much as I love the day-care center." Bolting across the room, she headed toward her bedroom. "Please go now, Luke. I need to be alone."

He heard the slamming of her bedroom door. For long moments, he stood, breathing heavily, surprised at the emotions he was feeling. The painting belonged to Casey. She had every right to sell it if she pleased. Yet he felt such anger inside, knowing she had to sell something she loved just to pay her bills. He stared around the lovely old room, filled with the things she and her grandmother had shared. Some of the color seemed gone from this place. But he couldn't decide if that was due to the loss of the painting or the absence of the beautiful young woman who filled this house with her vitality.

Luke walked slowly down the hall toward her bedroom. What was happening to him? Why did this damnably independent slip of a girl always make him experience so many different emotions? She made him so angry that he wanted to shake her. She made him laugh as no one else had ever made him laugh. She made him care. Care about things he didn't want to care about ever again.

He had vowed he'd never again fall into a woman's trap. He could still remember all the pain, the anger, the frustration he had experienced when Lyn walked out. Only a fool would ever risk it all again.

Standing outside her door a moment, he hesitated, wondering if he had the right to intrude on her privacy. He knocked. There was no response from within. Turning the knob, he pushed the door open.

A thin slice of golden moonlight spilled over the figure lying facedown across the bed.

"Casey." Luke sat on the edge of the bed and touched her shoulder.

The mattress sagged beneath his weight. Startled, Casey lifted her head. Tears glimmered on her lashes and rolled down one cheek.

"Go away, Luke. I do my crying in private."

His hand lingered on her shoulder. "So do I." It tore at him to see her hurt. It was as if he shared her pain; he could feel it as intensely as his own. He drew her up into his arms.

Her tears flowed fresh. "It isn't just the painting,"

she sobbed against his neck. "It's all the special things that seem to be slipping away. My parents. Gram. My chance for . . . Oh, Luke."

Luke heard the sigh from deep within her and felt the shudders she sought to control. He longed to comfort her, to ease her pain. Despite her warmth with children, he sensed that she was a very private person and that she was sharing something deep, something personal.

His hand moved up to her throat. She leaned up on one elbow, causing her hair to spill over one shoulder. Her hair was as soft as silk as it brushed his hand. Without thinking, he buried his face in her hair. He felt the need for her rising in him and banked the fire that flickered. He heard her sudden intake of breath.

His thumb caressed the cord at her neck. He wanted only to soothe the tension.

Tears shimmered on her lids, and one spilled over, trickling down her cheek. He bent his lips to her eye. He wanted only to kiss away the tears. He wanted only to hold her, to rock her in his arms, to make everything better. But the moment Casey was in his arms, everything changed. He could feel her warm flesh beneath the robe, and his hand stiffened.

At the tenderness of Luke's touch, she relaxed against him, melting into his embrace. Wrapping her arms around his waist, she clung to him. With her guard down, she was unprepared for the passion that suddenly took over her control.

His lips followed the trail of the tear along her cheek. For a brief moment, he lifted his head, studying her eyes. Then his lips covered hers in a searing kiss. Dazed at the heat which suddenly coursed through her body, she clung to him, returning the kiss. His lips were salty from her tears. With his teeth, he nipped her lower lip until she moaned and deepened the kiss.

He could feel the heat of her body. With a sort of madness taking over his control, he slid a hand inside the robe until he found her breast, firm and smooth. Lost in the kiss, he moaned and drew her down on the bed with him. All the while, his thumb continued to torment and arouse her taut nipple until she strained toward him.

She was on fire. Her body had become a mass of nerve-endings, aching for relief. His arm tightened around her, pressing her closer until she could feel the imprint of his body on hers.

There was no tenderness in him now. His body was hard, taut. His kiss was demanding, leading her higher, taking all she had to give. There was a fierce hunger in him that she found herself wanting to satisfy. She shared his needs, his desires. Beneath his shirt she could feel the pounding of his heart. Its wild rhythm matched her own. Her blood roared in her temples.

His hands gripped her convulsively, holding her for a brief moment against the length of him. Then, abruptly, he pulled her away, holding her at arm's length. Staring down at her, he was aware of the confusion in her eyes. Her lips were swollen from his kisses. Her hair tumbled about her shoulders. Her robe had parted, revealing seductive, translucent skin.

Gathering her robe about her, he tied the sash, all the while watching her eyes. He could read in them a slumberous, wakening passion.

"I hope you'll believe that I didn't mean this to happen, Casey."

She remained silent, unwilling to trust her voice.

"I'm sorry. I'll let myself out."

She continued to kneel in the middle of the bed, watching as he walked quickly from the room. She listened to the sound of his footsteps as he walked down the stairs. Then she heard the slam of the door. And then, as it had so often in the past, the silence of the old house closed around her.

Chapter Ten

"Here, Vern. Let me help you with that."

Casey, clad in faded jeans and a bulky sweatshirt, strained at one end of a heavy tree limb while Vern struggled with the other end. Everything had to be piled at the streetside curb for a special trash pickup arranged by the city. Judging by the growing pile of branches and debris, the storm had done much more damage than Casey had first assumed.

She was maneuvering her heavy burden around the corner of the house when suddenly a pair of hands appeared beside hers, easing the weight.

She turned, nearly colliding against his chest. "Luke. What are you doing here?"

For a moment he gave her a sheepish look. "I figured you'd need some help. So I'm here to offer my body for hire."

"Hmm." Unable to resist laughing at the implication, she lifted one eyebrow like a movie villian. Allowing her gaze to travel slowly up and down his trim figure, she said, "I'm sure I could find something useful for that body."

He grinned, delighted at her humor. "I intend to take you up on that."

"First," she said, deciding to play it straight, "you can help drag those broken branches over there. Everything goes on that pile. After that, we'll need to rake the flower beds. Think you can handle it?"

With a grin, he flexed a muscle for her benefit before bending to his task.

Danny bounded up beside Trouble. "I want to help, Casey."

"Good boy. See that trash barrel over there?"

Danny nodded.

"You can throw all the broken branches and twigs in there. Trouble will probably lend a hand . . . uh, I mean a mouth, if you toss him an occasional stick."

Giggling, Danny hurried to get to work.

"Hey, Casey," Vern called, picking up a pair of long-handled pruning shears, "how about some coffee?"

"Okay." She hurried indoors.

A short time later, she carried a tray laden with coffee, mugs, cream and sugar, and a plate of chocolate-chip cookies. For Danny there was lemonade. She had even added a dog biscuit for Trouble. Placing it on a picnic table, she called to her coworkers, who were eager to take a break.

"Umm. That's good," Vern murmured, wrapping his hands around a mug of steaming coffee. Peering into the trash barrel, he gave Danny a wink. "You're doing a fine job."

Danny beamed at the words of praise. Stuffing a cookie into his mouth, he picked up the glass of lemonade and drained it.

"Come on over here, Danny. I found something I bet you never saw before," Vern called, leading the little boy across the yard.

Luke watched as the old man dropped a hand around his young son's shoulders. The shaggy dog trailed happily behind.

"A day like this is so good for Danny," Luke mused, taking a long drink of coffee. "Everyone here has become the family he missed having."

Casey sat down on the rough seat and sipped her coffee in thoughtful silence. "Is that why you came today, Luke? To fill a need in Danny's life?"

Luke swung a leg over the bench and faced her across the picnic table. "Maybe that's part of it." He looked away a moment, watching the old man and little boy, bent over something near the fence. "We have so many needs. Sometimes they get all mixed up. I need to be a good father to Danny. But I also need to be good at my job. Sometimes the two are in conflict." His voice lowered perceptibly, and Casey saw his hands tighten around the mug. "And for a long time now, I've denied other needs in my life."

Across the yard, the old man chuckled, and the high-pitched sound of a little boy's laughter carried on the breeze. Luke watched them for long minutes.

"I used to think I'd be content to stay the way we were, just the two of us."

"And now?" Casey held her breath.

For what seemed an eternity, Luke stared into space. Then he just shrugged. "I don't know what to think anymore."

Her heart fell. Was Luke thinking of a reconciliation? Could that be the reason for Lyn's visit to Chicago?

Luke's gaze narrowed on her. Casey flushed under his scrutiny.

He frowned, deep in thought. The young woman across the table was such a contradiction. She wasn't married, and yet she was surrounded by children. A dedicated career woman who couldn't bring herself to charge enough to pay the bills. So tenderhearted, she took in every stray dog, cat or human who looked at her with big, sad eyes. Yet she sold a cherished possession without batting an eye. She made child-rearing look like fun, rather than the hard work he knew it must be.

Without realizing where his thoughts were leading, he spoke the words aloud. "Who are you, Casey Leary?"

She averted her gaze, disturbed by his piercing look. "I've come from a distant galaxy. Take me to your leader."

His frown was replaced with a grin. "Tell me about you."

"I like the people on your planet, both old and young. I especially like the handsome men of the species."

He laughed at her silliness.

Sobering, she said, "I love this old house, this yard filled with fruit trees and flowers. Yet I know someday it will have to come down, to make room for apartments or condominiums. And when that happens, I hope I'll be able to move on without regrets." She wrinkled her nose. "Well, maybe a few regrets. But I'll be able to live through it. I want to be independent, yet sometimes I think it would be nice to be taken care of." She shrugged. "When I was little, I thought I'd be a great actress, or a dancer. In college, I thought I'd like to be a journalist, a foreign correspondent, and travel the world, reporting on wars and famine and all the horrible things that fill our newspapers." She gave a little self-conscious laugh. "So here I am, still in my grandmother's old house in Chicago, taking care of other people's children, and, frankly, having the time of my life. I guess I'm a contradiction."

He reached a hand across the rough table top. At his touch she felt the familiar rush of blood at her temples.

"A very nice contradiction, Casey."

"Come on." She stood suddenly, determined to be sensible. "There's work to be done."

For the next several hours, they raked, hauled and carried, until all traces of the storm damage had been removed.

"Come on, Vern. I'll make some lunch," Casey offered.

"No, thanks," Vern called. "Maybe another time, Casey. I promised my sister I'd drive to her house today." He made a face. "She's determined to take me shopping for some new clothes. She says I'm beginning to look like a rag picker." He lifted an arm, displaying a jagged tear that ran the length of a seam. "This old shirt's good for at least another year. But I know Tess. She'll throw it out. And it's one of my favorites."

"Women," Luke said, winking at Casey. "Always trying to improve on nature. They always want to make their men better, don't they, Vern?"

"Yep," the old man agreed with a laugh. "Thank goodness. What would we do without 'em?" With a quick wave, he headed across the yard toward his home.

"Come on, Casey," Luke suddenly said, grabbing her hand. "Instead of having lunch here, I'm buying."

"Looking like this?" Casey glanced down at her stained jeans, then glanced at Luke and Danny, who looked equally grubby.

"I know a great place that won't throw us out."

They piled into the car, and Luke drove along the familiar streets of Chicago until they came to a small diner.

Inside, they inhaled the wonderful scents of onions and chili.

Casey glanced at the menu, then laughed. "Bet I know what you're having," she said to Danny.

"A hot dog."

She nodded. "Me too. With lots of chili and onions."

Luke ordered, and within minutes they hungrily ate hot dogs, catching the oozing chili and mustard with a napkin. The french fries were still sizzling when they were placed in front of them.

"Now this," Casey said, taking a long gulp of soda, "is a feast."

"Nothing but the best when I buy," Luke said expansively.

When they left the diner, Casey sighed. "I don't know about you two, but I'm stuffed. I think we'd better walk a bit."

Leaving the car, they strolled along the bustling sidewalk, peering into store windows, watching the throngs of people shopping. At a movie theater, they stopped to read the marquee.

"Children's matinee. A Disney double feature." Luke turned to Casey and Danny. "What do you say?"

They both nodded at once. Luke bought three tickets, and they hurried inside.

"I'll spring for popcorn," Luke offered.

Immediately, Casey and Danny nodded.

"I thought you two were stuffed," he muttered.

"That was before you mentioned popcorn," Casey said, nudging Danny with her elbow. "Come on, big spender, you promised."

For the next several hours, they joined dozens of children in the magic of cartoons.

By the time they left the theater, dusk had fallen over the city. Streetlights were coming on. The crowds of shoppers had thinned to a few hardy souls waiting for buses and cabs. Danny, too tired to walk to the car, lifted his arms to his father. Luke cradled him against his big shoulder and dropped his other arm around Casey.

"I liked Dumbo," Luke said, smiling down at her.

"Bambi is my favorite."

"I saw you crying."

"I always cry over Bambi."

"Did you enjoy yourself?" he asked softly.

"I loved it. I'd forgotten how much fun Saturday matinees are. The kids were such an enthusiastic audience. Didn't you love it when they cheered?"

He grinned at her. "Oh, yeah. And I loved it when that kid behind me jumped up cheering and forgot he was holding a box of popcorn. I think I'll be picking popcorn out of my hair for a week."

When they reached the car, Luke gently placed his sleeping son on the back seat. Luke and Casey shared a companionable silence on the drive to her house.

This had been one of the best days of her life. It had begun like so many Saturdays—with mundane chores. But Luke had transformed it into something special. Who would have ever believed that dour, hostile man she had met just short months ago would be the cause of so much happiness?

Casey turned to watch him as he drove. Her heart rose in her chest. The thought came suddenly, unbidden.

I love him.

The thought was so overwhelming that she turned and stared out the window, watching the montage of buildings and colors and lights speed past.

She wanted to tell him, to share this wonderful knowledge. But she couldn't. What would a man like Luke say if she were to blurt out the truth? That's very nice, Casey, but you see, I have this ex-wife to deal with right now, and a little son who needs me to be strong, and all these problems with my job, and I just don't have room for any more complications.

She couldn't tell him yet. But Casey hugged the

knowledge to her heart. She knew she loved him. Right now, that was all that mattered.

As he turned the car up the sloping driveway of her house, Danny stirred. Sitting up, he rubbed his eyes.

"Are we home, Dad?"

"Not yet. We're at Casey's house."

Kneeling, he poked his head over the front seat. "This was fun, Dad."

Casey tousled his hair. "It was a great day. Thank you both. I can't remember when I had more fun."

"Can we come in for chocolate-chip cookies?" Danny asked.

Casey laughed. "Sure. I think I have a few left." She glanced at his father. "Want to?"

"Okay. They should sit well with chili dogs and popcorn. The perfect ending to a perfect day."

Laughing, the three of them walked up the steps to the front door. Inside, Danny ran off in search of Trouble.

"Try my bedroom," Casey called after him. "He hates to be left alone. He's either cowering in my closet or sleeping on my bed."

"You let that monster up on your bed?" Luke grabbed a handful of her hair and stared down into laughing eyes.

She laughed as she led the way to the kitchen. "He's such a coward. My room seems to give him some comfort."

Danny and Trouble trailed them into the kitchen, where Casey got down the cookie jar and three glasses of milk.

"You were right, Casey. He was up on your bed."

"He doesn't understand that he's big and hairy," Casey explained. "He thinks he's a tiny lapdog."

"Why doesn't Duchess keep him company when you're away?" Danny asked, picking up a cookie.

"Cats are very independent. She just curls up on a window ledge and ignores him."

"Poor Trouble," Danny murmured, petting the dog. When he saved the last bite of his cookie for Trouble, Casey glanced meaningfully at Luke.

"That's nice of you to share with Trouble. He loves chocolate-chip cookies."

"Can we have another?"

Casey nodded. "If it's all right with your father."

Luke grinned. "Go ahead, Danny. I think I'll take two, too."

When they had finished every crumb, Casey walked Luke and Danny downstairs to the front door. Enveloped in a warm, family feeling, she lifted Danny and gave him a kiss before turning to his father.

"It's been a wonderful day, Luke."

"For me, too." He stared down at her, wishing he could take her in his arms. The thought of her soft, willing body made his pulse quicken.

As if sensing his thoughts, she leaned toward him, longing to touch him.

"When we get home, Dad, do you think the phone will still be ringing?"

Puzzled, Casey glanced down at Danny, then back up at his father. "What is that about, Luke?" She noted the same sheepish look on his face that she had detected earlier that morning.

"The phone, Dad. 'Member?" Innocently, Danny

turned to Casey. "This morning, the phone rang and rang. Dad said we couldn't answer it. Then we got dressed and drove over here."

Lyn! How could Casey have forgotten so easily? Lyn was still in town and trying to see her son. And to avoid her, Luke had brought Danny here, where Lyn couldn't find him. This wonderful day hadn't just happened because of their sheer joy in each other's company. This whole day was part of Luke's plan to avoid his ex-wife and rob her of her chance to see her son. It wasn't reconciliation he was thinking about. It was revenge.

Luke took one look at Casey's stricken face and caught her by the shoulder. "Casey, let me explain . . ."

"No, Luke." Her voice felt strangled in her throat.

"But I . . ."

"Please go. It's been a long day." She glanced down at Danny, standing apart, watching them in perplexed silence.

"Your son must be tired. I know *I* am." Her voice lowered, so that only Luke heard the rest. "Tired of your lies. Good night."

Spinning on his heel, Luke picked up his son and stalked out the door.

Casey stood in the doorway until the silver car disappeared into traffic. In the glare of the porch light tears filled her eyes and glittered on her lashes. With an angry gesture, she brushed them away with the back of her hand. No more tears over Luke Pierson, she thought with a fury. This was the last time she would allow him to use her. All those sweet lies. How could she have believed them?

Love. Just a little while ago, she was telling herself she was in love with him. When would she ever learn? Every time she thought she was in love, she got hurt. Never again. She had no idea what love was. But she knew one thing. She was definitely never going to allow herself to love a man like Luke Pierson.

Chapter Eleven

Late-morning sun slanted through the tall, floor-to-ceiling window of the sitting room. The figure on the white sofa sprawled, face down, hair fanned out about her head and shoulders like a veil. The colorful afghan had slipped to the floor, revealing her delicate white lace teddy. One foot rested over the arm of the sofa. The other dangled over the edge, hanging in space. One arm was wedged between her body and the back of the sofa. The other was thrust over her head. She lay, limp and unmoving, like a discarded rag doll. Above her, on the back of the sofa, a cat lay purring its contentment in a shaft of sunlight.

A ringing shattered the stillness. The figure stirred. On the second ring, the figure rolled into a fetal position. Still the ringing went on, until, no longer able to ignore it, she sat up. The arm that had been pinned beneath her began to waken with the stabbing of a million needles. Dazed, she reached for the phone.

"Hello."

There was no response. She stared at the instrument. The ringing continued. She lifted her head as the dog lumbered to its feet. It was the doorbell, she realized.

With a toss of her head, she shook the hair back from her face. It cascaded in wild tangles about her neck and shoulders. Picking up the silk kimono from the arm of a chair where she had tossed it the night before, she tied the sash and padded barefoot down the stairs. Trouble bounded ahead of her.

She peered through the window and was startled to see Luke's face staring back.

"What do you want?" she said.

She threw open the door. Luke, clad in dark slacks and a dark sweater beneath a tweed sport coat, had to back away to allow the big dog to pass.

"And a cheery good morning to you. So this is how you look when you wake up." Feeling his pulse race, Luke's gaze slid over her.

"I was sound asleep. What are you doing here?" She didn't even make an attempt to keep the anger from her tone.

"We're going to have to do something about your attitude in the mornings, Miss Leary. You look like you just sucked a lemon."

"I'm not in the mood for jokes, Luke."

"Are you in the mood for breakfast? I'm making it," he said, picking up a large grocery bag from the porch.

"No. Go make it in your own kitchen."

"I can't," he said, sweeping past her and heading for the stairs.

Trying to get her bearings, she slammed the door and hurried to keep up with his quick steps.

"Why can't you?"

He turned at the hallway and gave her a disarming smile. "Because there's no one to eat it. What's the fun of going to all the trouble of making something if there's no one to enjoy it?"

For the first time, she became fully alert. "Where's Danny?"

Luke walked to the kitchen and began removing items from the bag. "He's with his mother."

Casey froze. "When did she . . ." She licked her lips. "When did you decide to let her see Danny?"

He began rummaging through cupboards, rattling pots and pans. "Several days ago, an angelic little voice kept nagging me about doing the right thing, the generous thing. Finally, to silence it, I decided to give it a try."

She stood very still. His back was to her as he fiddled with the dials of her stove. She felt a rush of conflicting emotions. Several days ago? So he had listened to her after all. She should feel elated. But if he had made his decision then, why was he avoiding the ringing telephone yesterday? Whom could he be avoiding, if not Lyn?

Lyn. Could this be a first step in a reconciliation? For a moment her heart stopped. Then, brushing her fears aside, she reminded herself that the most important consideration was Danny. He had the right to know and love both a mother and a father. And Luke had just taken a very important step for Danny's sake.

Luke turned from the stove and studied her a moment. Then, with a wicked smile he said, "You'd better go put some clothes on. If you stand around in that outfit much longer, I won't be responsible for what I do."

For the first time, Casey realized how she must look. Fleeing Luke's burning gaze, she hurried from the room, missing the warm smile that lit his features.

Casey stood beneath the stinging spray of the shower, willing herself fully awake. The night before had seemed endless as she had paced the room doing battle with her highly strung emotions. What had Luke Pierson done to her? One minute, he made her so happy she thought her heart would burst. The next, she was so down, nothing could lift her spirits.

When she emerged from her bedroom she was dressed in a camel skirt and jacket with an amber silk shirt that nearly matched her eyes. Her hair fell soft and loose, with traces of dampness still clinging to little tendrils that curled about her neck and brushed her cheeks.

"Try the orange juice. It's fresh." Luke handed her a glass, and she drank.

"Wonderful."

Her flawless skin needed no makeup, he noted. She looked fresh, clean. She made him feel the same.

"Here." He held her chair.

Clattering pots and pans, he produced two plates heaped with fried potatoes, sausages, eggs scrambled to perfection, and lightly toasted French bread.

"Just like my mother used to make," he boasted.

Casey shook her head. "You'd better get a job cooking for a football team. The two of us will never eat all this."

"Want to bet?" With a grin, he picked up a fork and began savoring the meal.

Casey tasted, smiled, then began enjoying it herself. The food was excellent.

"When's the last time you were served a breakfast like this?" Luke asked between bites.

"It's been years. At a little inn in Toronto. I took Gram up for a weekend." Casey smiled, remembering.

Over coffee in the sitting room later, Casey asked, "Did you really decide days ago to let Lyn visit Danny?"

Luke nodded.

"Then whose phone call were you avoiding yesterday morning?"

Luke's lips thinned to a frown. "One of our investors wanted me to accompany him to the drill site this weekend. He has a hard time taking no for an answer." Luke's eyes narrowed slightly. "Weekends are the only time I have exclusively for Danny. That's important for both of us. I tried to explain the same thing to Lyn. But she had only one more day in town."

Casey flushed, remembering how easily she had leaped to the wrong conclusion. "Luke, I'm sorry. I . . ."

Impatiently, he stood. "Come on. Let's clean up the mess I made in your kitchen. The day is young, and we have it all to ourselves."

"Don't you have any plans?" she asked as she picked up her cup and led the way.

"Umm. Yes, but I'm afraid you'll slap my face if I tell you what they are."

She glanced over her shoulder. Seeing his wicked grin, she said, "You're right. I will. And it so happens, I have a few plans of my own today."

"Are you telling me I have to leave?"

She handed him a dish towel. "That depends. I promised Patience I'd drive her downtown this afternoon. She has some shopping to do. I thought I'd buy her lunch."

"Mind if I tag along?"

Casey was pleased by Luke's offer. "Not at all."

If Patience was surprised to see Luke's car instead of Casey's van, she didn't show it.

"Well, Luke, how nice to see you." Patience glanced around. "Where's Danny?"

"He's visiting his mother," Luke said as he settled her comfortably in the back seat.

Patience gave Casey a wink, then sat back, enjoying their company.

As they drove toward the downtown area, the older woman indicated some of the shopping malls. "I know I could shop just as comfortably here, but there's something about downtown Chicago that has always excited me." The dark eyes sparkled as she took in the city's skyline. "So many new buildings keep rising. There's a youthful vitality, a brashness about the city. And yet," she said, wistfully, "there's a grace and beauty too, like a dignified great lady."

"A description that suits you as well." Luke pulled over to the curb where she indicated and assisted her from the car.

One eyebrow arched, she regarded him in surprise, then said to Casey, "This man has very good taste." She turned away. "I'll only be a few minutes."

"Take your time. We have all afternoon."

When Patience entered the store, Casey burst into laughter. "I think she was actually blushing."

"Maybe she isn't used to honest compliments," Luke said.

"Or being so gallantly treated by a handsome stranger."

"Handsome stranger?" He grinned. "Do you really think so?"

"Is that what I said? I meant to say loathsome strangler."

Putting his fingers around her throat, he growled, "I'll get you for that one, Miss Leary."

Luke parked the car and he and Casey waited outside the store for Patience. They were still trading banter when she emerged. Handing Luke her package, she began to walk along the street, with Casey and Luke in tow. She stopped at nearly every block—to visit the butcher, the bake shop, the dress shop, and the pharmacy.

By the time they had traveled two blocks, Luke's arms were filled with shopping bags and boxes. With her shopping and errands completed, Luke loaded her packages in the car and drove them several more blocks. When he pulled up to an elegant hotel, both Casey and Patience were surprised.

"I think you two ladies deserve lunch in the grand style." He offered them each an arm as he escorted them through the plush, quiet lobby.

In the center of the room was a fountain. Tastefully arranged around the room were small love seats and matching upholstered chairs. Waiters moved about with tea carts and trays of champagne. Along with these they were treated to delicate sandwiches, fruit, and cheese.

Casey excused herself, leaving Luke and Patience alone at the table.

Patience sighed in contentment. "My husband always brought me here whenever we came to Chicago. It was the highlight of our trip."

"What did he do?" Luke asked.

"He was a geologist for the U.S. Government. We must have lived in a hundred different places during his career. But somehow I always knew I'd come back to Chicago when we retired."

"How long ago did you return?" Luke passed her a plate of fruit.

Selecting several strawberries, she said, "Two years ago. I was feeling so alone in this big city." Her eyes reflected her sad memories. "I buried all the men in my life. My husband, son, grandson. I can remember thinking that I'd come home to die."

Luke's astonishment showed. "You, Patience?"

She nodded, and then her eyes lit up. "Then I met Casey. She was so warm, so vital. So filled with a zest for living. She asked me to help her with her projected day-care operation." The old woman laughed. "I'd never met anyone who seemed less apt to make a go of a business. But I had nothing but time on my hands, so I agreed. Thank heavens," she added with fervor. "My neighbors in the senior complex were so jealous when they found out that I was working." She looked away a moment, blinking away the mist that clouded her eyes. "That chance meeting with Casey saved my life. And everyone associated with her has a similar story."

When Casey returned to the table, she glanced from the older woman's beaming face to Luke's smiling features. These two seemed as comfortable together as two old friends.

When they arrived at Patience's apartment, Luke carried her packages in, then bent and kissed her tenderly on the cheek as he was leaving. Touching a finger to her cheek, she stood in the doorway waving until the car was out of sight.

At the car, Luke removed his tweed jacket and dropped it in the back seat. Warmed by the sun, Casey did the same.

"This has been quite a day."

"It isn't over yet." Luke gave Casey a smile. His gaze roamed appreciatively over the amber silk blouse.

"Just full of surprises, aren't you, Mr. Pierson."

"You haven't seen my place yet, have you?"

Casey felt a thread of alarm. Ignoring the prickly feeling, she shook her head. "No. You said Lake Shore Drive, didn't you?"

He nodded, and turned the car in that direction.

Luke drove to a tall building of gleaming glass and concrete. Giant pots planted with red geraniums stood at either side of the entrance. Handing the car keys to a doorman, Luke took Casey's arm and led her inside. A uniformed guard sat at a bank of monitors. He glanced up briefly, touched his hat, then resumed his careful watch.

A mirrored elevator whisked them to the twenty-third floor. Luke inserted his key and led Casey inside.

Her heels tapped on a gleaming white marble foyer. In the corner stood a contemporary glass-and-chrome clock, its pendulum swinging hypnotically back and forth. She walked across oyster carpeting, luxuriously thick. Her first impression was of light and space. The walls and ceiling were white. Two white sofas flanked an immense fireplace of white granite. The only color in the room came from a vivid contemporary painting in red, black, and white that hung above the fireplace. Two chairs, upholstered in red, black and white windowpane plaid, echoed the colors. Two steps up from the living room, a stark glass dining-room table was flanked by matching chairs. In the center of the table was a massive arrangement of red poppies and white daisies. The wall beyond consisted of floor-to-ceiling windows with a breathtaking view of Lake Michigan.

Casey hurried across the room.

"Oh, Luke. What a beautiful sight to greet you each day."

He stood beside her, his gaze locked on her. "I can't think of a more beautiful one."

She glanced up and, seeing his look, smiled. "I meant the view of the lake."

"To each his own." He caught a strand of her hair and began twirling it on his finger. He itched to touch her face, to feel the smooth texture of her skin.

Casey felt the familiar rush of sensations that assaulted her whenever he was near. Backing up a step, she said, "Your apartment is. . . ."

"Sterile."

She stared at him a moment, then laughed. "Well, it is rather . . ." She strained for the right word. ". . . impersonal." Moving another step away, she said, "I don't see any pictures or personal mementos. There's nothing of you here, Luke."

"I rented this apartment furnished. I had no idea how long I'd be here, or even whether I'd stay." Swiftly he changed the subject. "How about some wine?"

Casey nodded and followed him into the kitchen. Gleaming white cabinets and countertops matched the white tile floor. Luke selected a bottle of wine from a well-stocked wine rack and twisted a corkscrew.

Crossing the room, Casey asked, "Where do you keep the glasses?"

"Up here."

Beside him, Casey reached up and retrieved two long-stemmed goblets. Luke inhaled the wonderful spring scent of her cologne and forced himself not to touch her.

Setting the glasses on a silver tray, Luke filled a crystal ice bucket with ice and placed the opened bottle of wine inside to chill. He carried the tray to the dining-room table, where he poured the wine and handed a glass to Casey.

Below them, the lights of the city were coming on. Out on Lake Michigan, the lights of boats danced across dark waves. On the horizon, white sails could be seen billowing against the darkening sky.

Standing at the window, Casey stared at the distant

lights. Without looking at Luke, she said, "This isn't what I expected."

He leaned a hip against the window and studied her. "What did you expect?"

"A very busy man with a young son." She shrugged. "I guess I thought there would be clothes and toys scattered about. Some kind of chaos, maybe. At least some dirty dishes in the sink."

He smiled at the confusion in her eyes. "Like the cartoon fathers who don't know how to boil water?"

She grinned. "I suppose. This is all so—perfect."

Luke set his drink down and moved closer. "Someone comes in to clean every day."

"Every day." She thought about her endless list of chores.

"And it's far from perfect, Casey," Luke said, moving closer still and running a finger along her cheek. "We sleep here. We occasionally eat here. But we really don't live here. I think of this as a—temporary shelter."

"Pretty elegant shelter." He saw her gaze sweep the room.

"Elegant and cold." Like some women, he thought. Beautiful faces, perfect bodies. But once you looked beyond that, there was nothing there. Nothing at all.

Reaching for her, he drew her to him, all the while watching her eyes. "You're so warm, Casey. Warm and vital. Everything you touch is warmed by you." Pressing his lips to her hair, he murmured, "Warm me, Casey. Touch me."

The depth of his request made her knees buckle. Clutching his arms, she swayed against him. His kiss was gentle, tasting the wine on her lips. His fingers roamed her silk-clad back, shooting sparks along her spine.

Drawing her closer, he changed the angle of the kiss and took it deeper. Her blood roared in her temples. They were alone in his apartment, and she knew she should be wary. But her mind wouldn't function. She was aware only of the man whose lips brought such pleasure. She clung to him with a desperate need.

Looking down at her, he stared into cat's eyes—soft, glowing in the dim light. In those eyes he could read all her confusion. And something else. Desire.

"My God, Casey. How I want you. I can't deny it any longer." He crushed her to him, his lips taking hers with a fierceness that stunned her.

She answered the kiss with equal strength. Her fingers luxuriated in his hair, drawing his head down. Her blood heated. Her hands coaxed.

He allowed her all the secret tastes of his mouth before drawing away to her throat. She heard him moan her name, or thought she did, as his lips probed her neck and the little hollow between her throat and shoulder. He followed the scent of her cologne and brought his lips lower still to the cleft between her breasts.

Not content to kiss her, his fingers roamed her back and sides, luxuriating in the soft silk that only enhanced the satin skin beneath. With his thumbs he grazed her breasts and felt her sharp intake of breath. Covering her lips with his, he continued to plunder her mouth while his thumbs stroked. Raw hunger became a desperate, driving need. Casey gasped aloud and arched herself in his arms. His thighs brushed hers. With his hands, he drew her hips firmly against his, making them both aware of his arousal.

With his lips still covering hers, Luke lifted her in his arms and carried her to his bedroom. Locked in his embrace, Casey felt as if she were floating. He lowered her to his bed and lay beside her, gathering her into his arms.

Nipping her lower lip between his teeth, he tugged until she begged for his kiss. Twining her fingers through his hair, she brought his head down until his lips covered hers. Her hands roamed his back and chest until, hungry to feel his skin, she slipped her hands beneath his sweater. She heard him gasp at her touch.

His lips were warm and searching, moving over her face. He undid the buttons of her blouse, then brought his lips to the soft swell of her breast.

Casey became aware of a thundering heartbeat. Hers? Or his? His lips and fingers brought unbearable pleasure and the dull, throbbing ache of need. She was aware of the dark, musky scent of him, of lips that could be incredibly soft or demanding, of hands that could be tender or amazingly strong.

Luke was beyond thought. He had never known such a driving need. The lilac scent of her surrounded him. Her response to his touch drove him to a frenzy. Her lips, her fingertips aroused him as no one ever had. He felt her shuddering need. The need for her was a sort of madness.

The sound of the buzzer seemed to go on forever, while the figures on the bed were lost in their own passion. Slowly, painfully, Luke surfaced. For long moments he stared down at the woman in his arms. Then, almost in slow motion, he reached over to the night table and touched a button.

"Yes?"

The voice of the guard floated through the intercom. "Your son is here, Mr. Pierson. With his mother."

He took a long, shaky breath. "Thanks, Dave. Send them up."

For long moments the only sound in the room was their labored breathing. Sitting up on the edge of the bed, Luke ran a hand distractedly through his hair.

Awkwardly, Casey fumbled with the buttons of her blouse. Her skirt was twisted up around her hips. Wriggling off the bed, she turned away.

He caught her hand and forced her to face him. His voice was low, angry. "I'm sorry, Casey."

She stared at him a moment in silence, then turned away. With as much dignity as she could manage, she crossed the room to the bathroom. Closing the door firmly, she pressed her heated forehead against the cool tile.

Chapter Twelve

With trembling hands, Casey washed her face and ran a comb through her tangles. Her purse was somewhere in the foyer. Or had she tossed it on a sofa? It didn't matter. There would be no chance to repair her makeup.

In the mirror, wide amber eyes looking too big for her face stared back at her. Her lips were still swollen from Luke's kisses. She stared at her reflection, wondering if what she had just shared with Luke would be obvious to anyone looking at her.

Lyn was his wife. Ex-wife, Casey reminded herself sternly. Lyn had known him intimately. She would have to be aware of the tension in him. If she still cared enough to look.

Hearing the door chime, Casey squared her shoulders and walked down the hallway, prepared to meet the mystery woman.

"Dad. I'm home."

Casey heard Danny's high-pitched voice as the door was thrust open. She heard his running steps on the marble floor, the sound of childish laughter as she envisioned Luke catching him up in his arms.

"I'm glad. I missed you." Luke's voice was deep, rich with emotion.

After a moment of silence, his voice changed. The carefully controlled anger of Luke's tone stopped her in the doorway.

"I thought you wanted him to spend the night."

"My plans changed. I have—an appointment."

For a moment, Casey's heart plummeted. From her vantage point, she could see that Lyn was everything she had imagined—and more. She was nearly as tall as Luke. Willowy, Casey thought, with ash-blond hair pulled into a graceful knot on top of her head. Cool blue eyes were dramatically outlined. High cheekbones gave her an aristocratic bearing. The dress and cape in sapphire jersey knit were stunning high fashion.

"Hey, Casey." Spotting her, Danny ran to her. "Look what Lyn bought me."

"Lyn?" Luke's strangled sound brought Casey's head up sharply.

"My agent was there," Lyn said quickly. "I didn't want Danny to call me mother in front of him. So I told him to just call me Lyn. Do you mind?"

Luke's hand clenched at his side as he silently watched her.

Danny held up a big brown stuffed dog for Casey to

see. "I told her all about Trouble, and how I sleep on him sometimes. So she got me this for my bed."

Casey knelt down to look at the toy. "Bet I know what you've named him."

"Little Trouble," Danny said with a wide smile.

"Now we'll have double trouble." She laughed, hoping to ease the tension. "I hope he doesn't get into as much mischief as Big Trouble."

"So you're Casey," Lyn said, walking closer.

Casey stood, feeling at a distinct disadvantage. Awkwardly, she offered her hand. "Hello, Lyn. It's nice to meet you."

"Danny told me all about you. He makes you sound like Mary Poppins."

Casey met the ice-blue stare and was shocked at what she could read there. Fear. Uncertainty. The faintest tremor of lower lip before Lyn gave Casey a tremulous smile. This cool, sophisticated woman was nervous. And it was obvious that she felt completely out of her element with her own child.

"Will you get a chance to visit often?" Casey asked.

Lyn shook her head. "Most of my work is in New York now." She brightened. "Although my agency thinks they may have found me a small part in a movie. If it clicks, I'll probably move to the Coast."

"Sounds exciting." Casey glanced at Luke, who stood to one side, watching them without expression.

"Well, it's a lot of hard work." Lyn's eyes darted from her son to Luke, then back to Casey. "But I'm determined to make it. It's what I've always wanted."

"Then I wish you luck." Casey realized as she spoke that she really meant those words. This woman had walked away from marriage and motherhood for the slim chance at celebrity. Casey hoped that someday it would all seem worth it.

"Well." Lyn sighed, forcing a bright smile. "Come give me a hug, Danny."

Bending stiffly, she opened her arms. The little boy stepped into her embrace. When he tilted his face and reached his lips to hers, she managed to turn her head slightly, accepting a kiss on her cheek.

Standing, she ruffled his hair. "I'll keep in touch. And—send you some pictures, so you don't forget what I look like."

"Okay." Danny turned. "Can I get out of my good clothes now, Dad?"

Luke glanced down at his son and nodded.

As her son left the room, Lyn took a deep breath and looked resolutely at Luke. "Thanks for letting me see him. I wasn't sure you'd agree. It was—decent of you. Probably more decent than I would have been in your place. I wish you all the best. I'll—be in touch."

"I hope you find what you're looking for, Lyn." Luke's voice was toneless.

"Thanks. I wish you the same."

"I already have."

She raised an eyebrow, then turned toward the door. The cape swirled dramatically around her. With her head high, she opened the door and walked out. It closed behind her with a soft click.

For what seemed an eternity, Luke and Casey stared at the door in silence. The only sound in the room was the tick of the clock.

Moistening her lips with her tongue, Casey broke the silence. "Are you sorry I talked you into this?"

He was staring at her strangely. He shrugged. "No. I'm glad. Really glad, Casey. For Danny's sake and for mine."

Maybe he'd forgotten how stunningly beautiful Lyn was. How glamorous. Casey felt a knife turn in her heart. Maybe he was remembering all the good times they'd shared. Forcing a bright smile she didn't feel, she said, "I'd like to go home now."

Luke nodded. "I'll get Danny."

Casey stood at the wall of glass, watching the shimmering lights of the city below. She should be relieved that Lyn and Danny's arrival stopped her from doing something she'd regret. But she wasn't. Hugging her arms about herself, she fought the hollow, empty feeling and swallowed the lump in her throat.

"You're looking tired. Why don't you take a few days off?" Patience plunked herself into the chair across from Casey's desk.

"Who'd take care of all this?" Casey indicated the piles of bills littering her desk top.

"I could handle it. I used to administer an entire school and its annual budget. I think I could manage a handful of youngsters and this measly stack of bills."

Casey sat back a moment, staring with new interest at her old friend.

"Why didn't you ever offer your services before?"

Patience lifted her shoulders in a shrug. "As I recall, I wasn't much in the mood for living, let alone taking on any responsibility. Besides, it was your show. I didn't want to butt in."

"If you were—running the show, what would you do differently?" Casey dropped her pen and folded her hands.

"Not much. I think your basic ideas are sound. I agree that older people seem more tolerant of children. And the people you've hired are well qualified. But I don't think you're charging nearly enough to cover expenses." Patience leaned forward, as if to emphasize her words. "And I'd hire someone to replace my neighbor, Marion."

"Why?"

"'Cause she loves to cook. So I'd let her take over the kitchen, and hire someone else to work with the children. I think your idea of letting each of us take our turn at lunch duty is a mistake. Some of us," she said, staring pointedly at Casey, "don't have much talent in the kitchen and ought to stay away from it completely."

"Are you saying you don't approve of the lunches I've been making?"

"Casey," she said with the hint of laughter in her tone, "you're lucky those kids are too young to rebel. Peanut butter sandwiches are not my idea of a great lunch."

Casey laughed. "And all this time I just thought no one was hungry when I made lunch. You should have told me sooner."

"Well, what do you say?" Patience persisted. "Want to get away for a while?"

Casey gave her a grateful smile. "It's tempting." She

was struck by an odd thought. "A fortune cookie said I'd be taking a long trip."

"Just say the word." Patience stood and crossed the room. As she opened the door, the phone rang. Casey thanked her, then answered it.

"Casey?"

She felt the familiar pull at the sound of Luke's deep voice. "Yes?"

"We've struck it." She could hear the tremor of excitement in his voice.

"Oil?" Her own voice was strangely high-pitched.

"Yes. They just called from the drill site." She could almost feel the energy through the telephone line. "I have to drive out there now. I'm afraid I'm going to be late. Would you mind keeping Danny until I get back?"

"No. Of course not. Oh, Luke," she breathed. "I'm so happy for you."

"I'll tell you all about it when I get back. And Casey"—his voice thickened with emotion—"thanks for being there for Danny."

For long moments after she hung up, she sat staring off into space. Having found oil, would Luke now move on to a new location? He was, after all, trying to build up a small company. He had to keep searching for precious oil.

Mentally shaking herself, she hurried from the office. It was her turn for lunch duty.

"As long as we have some time to ourselves," Casey said, parking the van, "why don't you and I explore the attic?"

"Oh, boy! Let's go."

Danny skipped up the stairs to Casey's rooms. In the hallway, she opened a narrow door which revealed a second set of stairs to the top floor of the house.

She hadn't been up here in more than a year. Turning on the light switch, they climbed to the musty attic. A bare lightbulb dangled from a cord. Cobwebs shimmered in the glare. An old rocker leaned against the wall. Beside it stood a steamer trunk. There were framed portraits of ancestors long forgotten. An album, its cover missing, spilled yellowed photographs on the floor.

Casey pointed to the sloping ceiling. "When I was little, my dad used to bring me up here during a rainstorm to watch the lightning, and listen to the patter of rain on the roof. On gray winter afternoons I'd sit by the window and dream of what I'd be when I grew up."

Danny propped his chin on his hands and stared out the window, pressing his nose to the glass. "I can see everything from up here." He turned. "Wow! A rocking horse." Danny climbed on the back of a wooden, hand-painted horse. His face showed his pleasure. Climbing down, he picked up a baseball and mitt. "Are these yours?"

Casey examined the mitt, then handed it back to him. "These belonged to my brother, Pat. See this?" She showed him the names scrawled on the ball. "These were all his teammates on the neighborhood baseball team that won it all that summer. He was the pitcher. He struck out the toughest kid on the block. Boy, was I proud of him."

"How old were you, Casey?"

She knelt beside the little boy. "Six. I was the envy of all my classmates because the hero of the day carried me home on his shoulders." She glanced down at the ball and mitt. "Would you like these, Danny?"

"You mean I can keep 'em?"

"I think Pat would like you to have them. I know I would."

"Thanks, Casey." He turned. "Hey, look at this old doll."

He picked it up, and the arm fell off. Laughing, Casey showed him how the arm fitted into a little slot. "This arm was always coming off. She was my favorite doll, though. Probably because she wasn't exotic or beautifully dressed. I could drag her around without worrying. Something was always broken on her. And I always knew I could fix it."

"Was this your bed, Casey?" Danny touched a wooden cradle, which rocked gently.

She ran a hand lovingly over the smooth wood. "Yes. It was used for me and all my brothers. And for my mother before that. And her mother before her."

"It must be real old," he said with a trace of awe.

"Yes." Casey felt her throat tighten.

"Why don't you take it down to the nursery?"

Kneeling, she touched a hand to it, watching the gentle rocking motion. "I really should. I suppose it's silly to save it. But I always thought . . ."

She tried to swallow the lump in her throat.

"Casey."

At the sound of Luke's voice, she turned. He was

standing in the doorway, watching her. How long had he been there? she wondered.

"Dad. This is the attic. Wouldn't it make a great bedroom? Look." Danny pointed out the dormer window. "I could fall asleep watching the stars. And Casey said rain sounds better up here." Turning around, he added, "And look at all this great junk Casey saved. I could have my own rocking horse. And her brother's baseball and mitt, and . . ."

"Okay." Luke held up a hand and smiled, but his gaze remained on Casey. A hint of unshed tears glimmered in her eyes.

"Why couldn't you and me marry Casey and live here? Then I wouldn't have to leave here every night and go back to the 'partment. And you'd laugh all the time, like you do when you're with Casey. And not stare out the window with that look on your face." His voice raced on. "You could come up here with me sometimes and watch the stars and listen to the rain. What do you say, Dad?"

Shocked into silence, Casey could only stare at the little boy. Glancing at Luke, she could feel his stiff withdrawal.

Luke's voice was gruff. "I'd say you're wound up like a top. Come on, Danny. Let's get going." He glanced down at the baseball and mitt. "Leave that here. It belongs to Casey."

Danny's lower lip quivered. "She said I could have it."

"Okay." Luke's tone softened. "Come on. It's late."

Casey glanced down at the tattered doll in her arms. Embarrassed, she set it down, then stood, brushing the dust from her jeans. She followed them down the stairs and snapped off ...e light.

Outside, Trouble bounded around the yard while Danny climbed into the car. Luke paused on the porch. Beneath the grime, he looked exhausted.

"Did they find oil?" Casey asked.

His eyes lit with enthusiasm. "Yes. Not a gusher, but a darn good deposit. It'll make us a good return on our investment."

"I'm glad, Luke."

"Casey." He touched her arm. Instantly, she felt the shock waves. He glanced at the boy in the car, then back to her. "Thanks for keeping Danny."

"I didn't mind. We had a great time."

His voice became gruff again. "Good night."

"'Night."

He studied her face and seemed about to say more. Without a word, he turned and walked stiffly to the car.

"Luke Pierson stopped by while you were out." Patience looked up from Casey's desk and handed her several messages. "We had a nice little visit."

Casey's head came up sharply. She was always suspicious when Patience tried to act casual. Gruff and blustery was more her style. Studying her old friend's face carefully, she decided this time she must have been wrong. There wasn't even a hint of mischief in those black eyes.

"What did he want?"

"Oh, mostly to arrange for a baby-sitter for a few days. I told him I was available."

"A baby-sitter? He's going away for a few days? Where?"

"Dallas, I believe. To report on the new oil well."

Casey's heart fell. So she had been right. Luke was planning to move on.

"Umm." Casey leafed through the messages, trying to look uninterested. "You didn't mention to him I'm taking a few days off, did you?"

"We were busy discussing his plans." Patience hurried across the room. "Oh. Vern said not to worry about picking up all your employees while you're gone. He's been looking forward to driving that shiny new van."

"Good. Thanks, Patience."

With her hand on the knob, the older woman turned. "All packed?"

"Just about. I'll finish tonight. I'd like to be on the road as soon as you get here tomorrow."

"Did you phone your brother to tell him you're coming?"

"Yes. I haven't seen him and his wife since last Christmas. If I don't hit much traffic, I should be there by dinnertime tomorrow." She looked at the paperwork on her desk. "If you don't need me for an hour or so, I'd like to finish up all this and leave you with a clean desk."

Patience grinned. "You're talking to an old workhorse. When you come back that desk will still be clean."

The day, like all the others, flew by in a rush of children's laughter and spilled milk and the sound of voices throughout the house.

By late evening, Casey had taken a long bath, washed her hair, and slipped into red satin jogging shorts and a white satin tank top for sleeping. Her suitcase lay ready near the door. A map of Michigan was spread open on the kitchen table. With a red pen Casey had traced the route to her brother's home.

The ring of the doorbell punctuated the silence. Trouble's head came up. Casey grabbed up her kimono and hurried down the stairs. She had asked Vern to stop by for the key to the van.

Peering out the window, she paused in the act of slipping her arm into the sleeve. It wasn't Vern's face staring back at her. It was Luke's.

"I was expecting Vern," she mumbled, opening the door.

"Do you always give him the pleasure of seeing you like that? I hope he has a strong heart."

Casey glanced down in embarrassment and finished pulling on the kimono. Tying the sash with a flourish, she said, "There. All neat and proper."

"I wasn't complaining," Luke said with a smile. "I liked it better without the robe. Are you going to invite me in?"

She blocked the doorway, crossing her arms over her chest in a gesture of defiance. "No. I . . ."

"But we have things to talk about."

"We have nothing to say, Luke."

He stared at her a moment, and she was reminded of the first time she had seen him—tense, threatening, looking as much like a rogue as any pirate in her children's books.

Sweeping past her, he hurried up the stairs.

She bounded after him, hissing, "I want you to go, Luke."

At the top of the stairs, he glanced at the suitcase. "Patience said you were going somewhere."

"I suspected she'd mentioned it. I'm going to my brother's house in Michigan. I thought I'd get away for a few days. I've been thinking that I'm ready for some changes in my life. Now, if you don't mind, I still have a lot to do."

"Why?"

"Why what?"

"Why are you ready for some changes?"

She frowned. "I've been thinking that maybe I've been holding onto the past too long. Gram's house, her things, the things from my childhood. Maybe it's time to move on." Her voice hardened. "Or grow up. It seems to me there were things I wanted to do, places I wanted to see. You once talked about taking risks. Maybe that's what I need."

"Good idea. Changes, I mean." He seemed suddenly to be in a wonderful mood. "Flying?"

"Driving. I'm going to use Vern's car. He's taking my van."

He stood looking down at her. "The only time I get to see you alone is here at night. There are so many people in your life, Casey. At times this place is so cluttered with people and animals, I feel like I'm at the zoo."

"Are you here to issue a complaint?"

"Yes." His voice had suddenly lowered.

"Put it in writing."

"Casey." He reached out a hand to her arm. The

instant he touched her, she jumped as though shocked by an electric current. "Sometimes I just want to be alone with you." He kept his hand on her arm, then moved it slowly upward over the silken sleeve. "There are things that need to be said, and I want to say them tonight, before I leave for Dallas."

She wanted to pull away. The nearness of him was a bittersweet pain. But his hands gripped her shoulders, holding her.

Luke's voice trembled with emotion. "After Lyn, I thought I could live without a woman in my life. That was one problem I didn't want to confront."

She looked up. His gaze locked on hers. "I figured if I just held onto all the hatred and bitterness, it would choke out any tender feelings that might linger. For a long time now, I've been perfectly content to keep things the way they were." His voice roughened. "When you urged me to let Lyn see Danny, I resented it. But now, I'm so grateful."

Casey tensed, trying to pull away. She didn't want his gratitude. She took a deep breath to keep her voice steady. "I understand. And now that you've seen Lyn again, you've been able to put aside the bitterness. I'm glad. I'm also glad you and Danny are learning to communicate your needs to each other. That's important. Especially now that you've had such success here and plan to move on."

"Talk about lack of communication. Casey, you haven't been paying attention to what I mean."

The doorbell rang, and Casey quickly turned away. "That will be Vern. He's here to pick up the key to my van."

Hurrying down the stairs, she handed the smiling man her keys, gave him a quick hug, and returned to where Luke was still standing, frowning at the interruption.

"Casey. We need to talk."

"I think it's all been said, Luke."

The telephone rang, and Casey turned away. Luke caught her, holding her still.

His voice was a low growl. "Don't answer that."

"I have to. It could be a parent calling to tell me that someone won't be in tomorrow."

"If they don't reach you, they'll phone Patience. Didn't you tell everyone that she would be in charge for a while?"

"Yes, but . . ."

"Let it go, Casey. We need to talk."

"Luke." She tried to pull away. "I can't ignore a ringing phone."

"All right. You leave me no choice." Picking her up, he tossed her over his shoulder and picked up her suitcase.

"Put me down, Luke," she shrieked, pounding her fists on his back. "What are you doing? Put me down."

Storming down the stairs, he dumped her unceremoniously on the front seat of his car.

"You've gone off the deep end, Luke. I swear, if you don't let me out of this car, I'll scream."

"Go ahead." He started the ignition and began driving away. "That story you gave me about your dangerous handyman was just a product of your wild imagination. And everyone knows Trouble wouldn't hurt a fly."

She had gone very still. "What do you intend to do—kidnap me?"

"Why not? You've already told everyone you're going away for a while. You have Patience to run the day-care center, and Vern to pick up your employees." He glanced over at her and she could see his smile in the darkness. "That was very accommodating of you, Miss Leary."

"You can't get away with this, Luke. I—I don't even have any shoes on. If you don't start explaining your crazy behavior this minute, I'll jump out of this moving car."

His eyes suddenly blazed with anger. His words were sharp. "We're finally alone. No distractions. Just sit here and listen."

Her eyes widened. With an angry gesture she began to reach for the door handle. With one arm, Luke forced her back against the seat and held her there. With a self-mocking laugh, he said, "You certainly haven't made any of this easy for me, Casey. Because of you, I've lost sleep, snarled at potential clients." He shook his head, and she heard his voice grow softer in the darkness. "But it has its compensations. I've just begun to realize what's meant by 'the love of a good woman.' You've made me face things about myself I didn't want to face. You've made me want to stretch and grow, to be better than I was. It's only now that I've begun to understand what was happening."

"Then maybe you'd care to enlighten me."

He sped along the highway and careened through a gate at Midway Airport. Casey watched in frozen silence as he drove past fleets of airplanes until he came to a stop beside a sleek, private jet.

He turned to her in the darkness. "After what Lyn did to us, I was convinced I'd never be able to love or trust again." His voice became as soft as a whisper. "But you made the impossible happen. I've fallen in love with you."

Her eyes widened. Tears brimmed and threatened to spill over. "Luke. I—can't ever give you a child. I . . ."

"That's old news, Casey. Lyn gave me a child. But she wasn't capable of giving love. Don't you see? You have an amazing capacity to love." His voice grew husky with emotion. "There's no denying it. I love you."

Love. He loved her. She couldn't seem to take it all in. Wordlessly she stared at him.

With a roguish smile, he reached into the back seat of the car and opened a foil bag. He handed her a five-pound box.

"What's this?"

"Open it."

She lifted the lid. Inside, nestled in waxed paper, were layers of fudge.

She sniffed, then lifted tear-bright, laughing eyes to his. "Peanut butter fudge? Oh, Luke," she sighed in mock wonderment, and her voice nearly broke. "How romantic."

He chuckled. "You once said you'd be a slave for peanut butter fudge. I decided to take advantage of your weakness and guarantee your love for me."

"You didn't have to buy my love, Luke. It was

already yours." She took a deep, shuddering sigh. "Oh, Luke. I've loved you for so long."

He caught her face between his hands and kissed her eyelids, her nose, her cheeks, and finally her lips. Warmth flowed through her, heating her skin and bringing a flush to her cheeks.

"I love you, Casey Leary. I need you. Danny and I both need you."

The tears that had threatened spilled down her cheeks, matting her eyelashes. With his thumbs, Luke wiped them away.

Handing her his handkerchief, he reached into the box of fudge and lifted a foil-wrapped lump. Opening it, he revealed a magnificent ruby ring, surrounded by small diamonds.

"Oh." Her eyes grew wide. "Luke, it's too extravagant. You need your money for your struggling company."

"Struggling." Luke's gaze grew tender. "Casey, where did you get that idea? I'm not struggling. I just needed to get back to some basic hard work. I was disillusioned with success. I needed some new challenges."

"This is all too much," she breathed, trying to understand.

His voice roughened. "That's why I was so angry when you sold a painting that you loved, just to make ends meet. Don't you see? I could have helped if I had known. The amount of money you got from that painting wasn't enough to make up for the loss of something you treasured."

"But I couldn't have asked for your help."

With his thumb and finger he lifted her chin. "No. I know you couldn't. Maybe that's just another crazy reason why I love you."

He glanced at the ring in her hand and gently held it to the light. "Do you like it?"

"I love it."

"I didn't want to take any chances," he said, slipping it onto the third finger of her left hand. "Remember what I once said about always having something in reserve? I thought if the fudge didn't work, maybe the ruby would. After all, you did say you'd rather have rubies."

She shook her head, as if she couldn't believe her eyes. "I'd better be careful what I say to you in the future. I may end up with something I didn't bargain for."

"You'll end up with me," he breathed against her mouth. "For a lifetime. You're coming with me to Dallas, Casey. We'll be married. You can see my ranch." He held her a little away from him. "Maybe you'll decide that there are a lot of strays in Dallas who could use some of your special kind of loving."

Opening the car door, he lifted her in his arms and carried her to the sleek plane. As a uniformed pilot held the door, Luke climbed the steps and swept her into the plush interior. The pilot discreetly disappeared, leaving them alone.

She stared around with an expression of awe. "Is this yours?"

"Ours," he whispered.

She shook her head. "Patience will never believe

this. Oh, Luke," she suddenly cried in distress. "What about Danny?"

"He's with Patience. Before I left, I gave him my word that you'd marry us. Now you have to make an honest man of me."

She stood, looking so small and delicate in her bare feet and silk kimono. "We couldn't disappoint Danny, could we?" At his smile she whispered, "I'll marry you both, and love you forever." Then a new thought struck her. "What about my house?"

He smiled at her. "We'll have to divide our time between Dallas and the Midwest for the next several years at least. Danny would never forgive us if we didn't build that bedroom at the top of your house. He wants to fall asleep watching the stars." He pulled her closer until she was crushed against him. "And I want to fall asleep for the rest of my life looking at you." His hands fumbled with the sash of the kimono, then found the satin shorts and tank top. "Miss Leary, you sleep in the most interesting things," he murmured against her lips.

The warmth began to spread, heating her flesh, melting her bones. His lips nuzzled her throat, then searched lower until they found the soft swell of her breast. She heard the whisper of silk and satin as her clothes slid to the floor. Her heart began hammering a wild, primitive beat as his lips and fingertips brought her once more to the edge of madness.

The plane sped along the runway, then soared skyward.

Luke glanced around. "Think there are any strays lurking around?"

She chuckled, a deep, throaty sound. "We have the place all to ourselves," she whispered against his lips. "Now, about that zoo . . ."

"Did I sound like I was complaining? Actually, I've always thought it would be fun to live with a dozen or so animals and the Marx Brothers and maybe a dash of Mary Poppins."

"Oh, you . . ."

"Shh. No more talking." His lips claimed hers, silencing her. Lifting her in his arms, he carried her toward the rear cabin of the plane. Setting her gently on the bed, he murmured, "We have so little time alone together. Let's not waste a single, precious moment."

WIN
a fabulous $50,000 diamond jewelry collection

ENTER
by filling out the coupon below and mailing it by September 30, 1985

Send entries to:

U.S.
Silhouette Diamond Sweepstakes
P.O. Box 779
Madison Square Station
New York, NY 10159

Canada
Silhouette Diamond Sweepstakes
Suite 191
238 Davenport Road
Toronto, Ontario M5R 1J6

SILHOUETTE DIAMOND SWEEPSTAKES ENTRY FORM

☐ Mrs.   ☐ Miss   ☐ Ms   ☐ Mr.

NAME _____ (please print)

ADDRESS _____ APT. #

CITY _____

STATE/(PROV.) _____

ZIP/(POSTAL CODE) _____

RTD-A-1

RULES FOR SILHOUETTE DIAMOND SWEEPSTAKES

OFFICIAL RULES—NO PURCHASE NECESSARY

1. Silhouette Diamond Sweepstakes is open to Canadian (except Quebec) and United States residents 18 years or older at the time of entry. Employees and immediate families of the publishers of Silhouette, their affiliates, retailers, distributors, printers, agencies and RONALD SMILEY INC. are excluded.

2. To enter, print your name and address on the official entry form or on a 3″ x 5″ slip of paper. You may enter as often as you choose, but each envelope must contain only one entry. Mail entries first class in Canada to Silhouette Diamond Sweepstakes, Suite 191, 238 Davenport Road, Toronto, Ontario M5R 1J6. In the United States, mail to Silhouette Diamond Sweepstakes, P.O. Box 779, Madison Square Station, New York, NY 10159. Entries must be postmarked between February 1 and September 30, 1985. Silhouette is not responsible for lost, late or misdirected mail.

3. First Prize of diamond jewelry, consisting of a necklace, ring, bracelet and earrings will be awarded. Approximate retail value is $50,000 U.S./$62,500 Canadian. Second Prize of 100 Silhouette Home Reader Service Subscriptions will be awarded. Approximate retail value of each is $162.00 U.S./$180.00 Canadian. No substitution, duplication, cash redemption or transfer of prizes will be permitted. Odds of winning depend upon the number of valid entries received. One prize to a family or household. Income taxes, other taxes and insurance on First Prize are the sole responsibility of the winners.

4. Winners will be selected under the supervision of RONALD SMILEY INC., an independent judging organization whose decisions are final, by random drawings from valid entries postmarked by September 30, 1985, and received no later than October 7, 1985. Entry in this sweepstakes indicates your awareness of the Official Rules. Winners who are residents of Canada must answer correctly a time-related arithmetical skill-testing question to qualify. First Prize winner will be notified by certified mail and must submit an Affidavit of Compliance within 10 days of notification. Returned Affidavits or prizes that are refused or undeliverable will result in alternative names being randomly drawn. Winners may be asked for use of their name and photo at no additional compensation.

5. For a First Prize winner list, send a stamped self-addressed envelope postmarked by September 30, 1985. In Canada, mail to Silhouette Diamond Contest Winner, Suite 309, 238 Davenport Road, Toronto, Ontario M5R 1J6. In the United States, mail to Silhouette Diamond Contest Winner, P.O. Box 182, Bowling Green Station, New York, NY 10274. This offer will appear in Silhouette publications and at participating retailers. Offer void in Quebec and subject to all Federal, Provincial, State and Municipal laws and regulations and wherever prohibited or restricted by law.

SDR-A-1

READERS' COMMENTS ON SILHOUETTE ROMANCES:

"The best time of my day is when I put my children to bed at naptime and sit down to read a Silhouette Romance. Keep up the good work."

P.M.*, Allegan, MI

"I am very fond of the quality of your Silhouette Romances. They are so real. I have tried to read some of the other romances, but I always come back to Silhouette."

C.S., Mechanicsburg, PA

"I feel that Silhouette Books offer a wider choice and/or variety than any of the other romance books available."

R.R., Aberdeen, WA

"I have enjoyed reading Silhouette Romances for many years now. They are light and refreshing. You can always put yourself in the main characters' place, feeling alive and beautiful."

J.M.K., San Antonio, TX

"My boyfriend always teases me about Silhouette Books. He asks me, how's my love life and naturally I say terrific, but I tell him that there is always room for a little more romance from Silhouette."

F.N., Ontario, Canada

*names available on request